Dreams In Ruin

Realm Wars Book 1

Josh Coker

Story Ninjas LLC

Table of Contents

Want to know when **Reflections Of Darkness: Realm Wars Book 2** goes live? Sign up to the mailing list![1]

Check out the Realm Wars Webpage[2] for book releases, lore, artwork and more!

---

1.   https://bookhip.com/JTLABZG

2. https://www.story-ninjas.com/realmwarsnewsletter

JOSH COKER

Chapter 1: Star Soup

The raiders attacked the child first.

Lightning flashed against the crimson treetops, illuminating the forest and revealing a group of fly-faced aliens; the Bush People. A chill trickled through Dash's veins. Although she'd never seen a buzzer up close, she had attended enough security briefings to know that she did not *want* to. The four-armed flesh eaters emerged from the bioluminescent foliage, equipped with primitive armor and technosticks. Rain drops fizzled against the taser-tipped weapons, as they converged on Astrea's position. Without thinking, Dash stepped in front of the girl. How in the realms would they get out of this mess? If Dash didn't come up with something quick, the raiders would turn her and the kid into star soup.

A heads-up display would have come in handy right about now. But that mucking explosion back at the lake ruins totally smoked her virtual vizard. Now she only wore the mask to keep the rain out of her eyes. And where exactly was the admin-drone? She sent that bucket of bolts back for help hours ago. Apparently Dash and Astrea were all on their own, which meant she'd have to improvise. Dash raised her hands. "We don't want any trouble."

The lead alien pointed at Astrea and buzzed orders in an indecipherable language. The other three attackers raised their technosticks and gave acknowledgement. Their voices grated against her ears like a garbled microphone. Were they wearing facemasks? Dash couldn't tell.

Astrea inched backward, "Miss Dash, I'm scared."

"See star cake, this is why we can't go following dragons into the woods."

"Yes, ma'am."

The buzzers pressed forward.

Dash picked up a fallen branch and pointed it at the closest assailant. "Back off bug breath." She swung the makeshift weapon wildly. *Snap.* The front section of the stick went limp, then fell into the mud. The alien cocked its head, looked to the forest floor and back at Dash, then thrust his technostick at her.

Dash bobbed her head out of the way.

The electrified fork came micrometers from her mask.

She threw the remaining piece of wood at him.

It missed, completely.

Of course.

She grabbed Astrea's hand, "Get your aft in gear kid!" she shouted, then pulled the child into the bushes.

As they weaved through the maze of glowing brush, Dash couldn't help but think how entirely astro this whole situation was. She was an automaton manager for star's sake. By all rights she should be sitting at her workstation, sipping coffee and reviewing code. Not getting chased by rag-wrapped aborigines in a dark forest during the middle of a thunderstorm.

Clack. Boom.

A bolt of lightning struck a nearby tree. Dash's foot snagged a root. Or, maybe it was a rock? She couldn't be sure.

Either way, she found herself falling face first into a thicket of thorns. As Dash braced for impact, she wondered how her boring life had come to this? Just yesterday she had been working on the server farms in the basement of the Hestia facility without a care in the world.

It was all those salvager's fault. She should have left that portal alone. Then she would have never gotten into this mess.

Dash scrambled to her feet and looked for Astrea.

Two of the buzzer's held the girl by the arms, while a third pointed a technistick at the child. The fourth approached Dash, weapon raised.

At that moment Dash realized one thing was for certain. She would never agree to babysit again.

Chapter 2: Pondering The Human Paradox

36 *HOURS EARLIER*
Humans are illogical creatures. Their entire youth is spent in school learning how to be good workers. By the time they reach adulthood, most have cultivated sufficient skills to enter the workforce. Once they're hired, they spend most of their waking hours at the job. Yet, the majority of their efforts are spent avoiding the work they came to do. Coffee breaks, smoke breaks, lunch breaks, afternoon walks, and bathroom breaks were just a few daily excuses that biosapiens used to evade the office. This list did not include fileday parties, company picnics, and office morale events, which seemed to occur at monthly rates. Considering how inefficient organics were when they actually did their tasks, it was remarkable that they accomplished anything at all. The fact that they managed to become the dominant organism in the galaxy completely defied logic.

MT-3R sped down the hall contemplating this paradox.

Clones and colonists from various organizations filled the walkways. Some chatted, while others reviewed holopads. The hoverton weaved past each obstacle like a hoverbike in traffic. Only one item remained on the daily checklist and the automaton was determined to accomplish it. Only a few hours remained to receive a ninety-seven percent efficiency rating for the week. As MT-3R turned the corner, a blinking light flashed on its internal communications display, indicating an incoming holo-message.

The machine paused, hovering in the air as it processed the information.

The subject line read:

LEVEL 1 PRIORITY

When the machine opened the message, its motivator thrust into overdrive. According to the report, Dig Site Four just went under full lockdown. As a level one priority, company protocol required the nearest admin-drone to assist the on-duty officer. The nav-display confirmed that MT-3R was closest to the executive suite. This was problematic. The machine would have to postpone its current task, in order to facilitate emergency actions. MT-3R helicoptered back and forth, weighing out the options. The call could take hours to complete, ruining any chance it had at achieving a ninety-seven percent productivity score. However, if the admin-drone passed the task to another automaton, the machine's impeccable compliance record would be tarnished.

After a micro moment of calculation, the hoverton concluded that accepting the priority call held the highest probability of resulting in the most ideal outcome. Perhaps the executive would not require any assistance at all, in which case MT-3R would be awarded participation points just for fielding the call. In any event, the admin-drone still had half the day to complete the other task.

"Affirmation: There is always time for one more task."

MT-3R spun around 180 degrees and raced back down the hallway.

On the way to the executive suite, the admin-drone listed likely causes for the lockdown. According to incident logs, despite occasional spiderbat infestations, nothing of significance had been reported near or around the dig sites since their inception. Nevertheless, unauthorized access could trigger an alarm. So would a major equipment malfunction. Fire drills could also activate a lockdown. Yes. Statistics favored this hypothesis by seventeen percent. The company often ran tests to gauge how personnel responded in emergency situations. Months had passed since the last drill, therefore it seemed reasonable that leadership had executed another one. MT-3R agreed with the concept of test runs. They provided opportunities to improve overall efficiency, which in turn bolstered unit productivity. Better metrics resulted in more funding. More funding resulted in new upgrades for administrative assets such as MT-3R. The machine could use a new motivator.

As the automaton approached the doorway, its audio receptors identified two voices arguing.

"We can't reactivate the portal," one voice said.

"That *does* sound like a problem," the other replied.

MT-3R slipped through the entryway and hovered toward the executive's desk.

"Those enviro-suits only hold so much oxygen. If we don't fix the slide screen soon, they could die."

Coolant trickled through MT-3R's components as it replayed the last words back through its processor.

Trapped?

DREAMS IN RUIN

Die?
This was not a drill.

Chapter 3: Don't Forget The Annual Training Slides

The possibility of a fire drill diminished to less than two percent. Apparently, this wasn't a test after all. It was a *real* emergency.

If the machine executed its duties according to protocol, MT-3R might receive more than an upgrade. On the other hand, if the admin-drone failed to perform adequately, it might find itself with a one-way ticket to the scrap pile.

Barcodes and bitmaps, the machine cursed inwardly.

When the hoverton turned the corner, its optical receptor identified the man sitting at the console as Cube employee 4382, Nat Buzznard. Executor Buzznard acted as the company lead officer at the Hestia facility. On the holocom in front of the executor, a three-dimensional image displayed a jowled man stroking thick mutton chops. Colonist 338, John Griff, the colony's Security Chief. MT-3R's identification chip compared each man's phenotype with an animal species, allowing the machine to easily differentiate between the two homo-sapiens. The Executor's frail features resembled that of a vulture, while the Chief's stocky frame matched a bulldog.

"How can we be of service to you, Griff?"

"I need a technician ASAP. Everything's on lockdown over here."

"I wish I could help, Griff." Buzznard slurped his drink through a straw. "But that's outside the scope of our contract. If you'd like to review the documentation—"

The Chief cut him off. "Contract? People's lives are at stake here."

The Executor raised a hand. "I'm sure we can work something out." He took another swig of his drink. "I just wanted to be clear that this service does not fall under our pre-existing agreement."

The Chief's jaw visibly clenched. MT-3R's processor couldn't always interpret human emotions, but according to behavior patterns, there was an eighty percent chance that the Security Chief was not calm. The jowled man stood in silence shaking his head, then sighed.

"How much?"

The executor leaned in. "Well, given the unconventional circumstances, and the timeliness of this task, it will cost..." He pressed a few buttons on his holopad, "...double the normal amount."

The Chief's eyes went wide. "You contractors are worse than the blasted refugees. You might as well just feed our men to a pantra."

The gangly man pointed his cup at the holocom. "Don't focus on the cost, think about how much you'll save when you don't have to replace any salvagers."

The chief inverted his eyebrows. "Your compassion is overwhelming."

The Executor smirked. "I'm sending our best technician."

The holoimage blipped out of existence and Buzznard dialed a new number into the holocom.

The machine rang.

And rang.

And rang some more.

The Executor paced the room.

Eventually, the call went to holo-mail. "We're sorry but the subscriber you're trying to reach has not set up their holo-mail. Please call back later."

The Buzznard squeezed his cup so tight, the lid popped right off.

"Sun spit," he cursed. "Where in the realms is that girl?"

MT-3R didn't quite know how to respond. Organics had an obtuse way of reacting to chemical changes in their body. No exact protocol existed for dealing with emotions. "Query: Executor, can this unit be of any assistance?"

He stopped pacing, then turned around, as if he were surprised to see MT-3R. "Yes, hoverton." He raised a finger. "I need you to locate Dash immediately."

Dash?

The machine searched Cube personnel files. MT-3R never understood why biosapens referred to themselves by names other than their company designator. According to birth records on file, the name Dash was rare among humans. Particularly females. According to MT-3R's internal dictionary, the etymology of the word denoted a person of swiftness. It was also a symbol used to indicate a missing element. Within 1.3 seconds the admin-drone located a full dossier on the employee named Dash. *How obtuse, there was no last name.* An image of a young woman displayed. Due to privacy laws, her exact age was unlisted. However, MT-3R's processor estimated the woman was in her mid to late twenties. The remaining information was quite basic.

NAME: Dash
COMPANY DESIGNATOR: Employee 1-X
OCCUPATION: Automaton Management
ASSIGNMENT: Basement Server farms

"Clarification: You mean, employee 1-X, sir?"

He waved a hand. "Yes, 1-X. Dash, that's her."

MT-3R scanned through the rest of the document. The file provided little information. The admin-drone found this anomalous, as most employees had full background checks and additional details attached to their folders. Under the employment history section, it merely read, *Prior Military*. 1-X also held the highest performance record in the quadrant, and apparently won last year's ladder races.

A cursor flashed on the machine's internal display. Under annual training, the box read incomplete. Despite MT-3R's multiple holo-mail reminders, 1-X was the only employee who had not completed the annual refresher slides. This one individual caused the whole division's timeliness metric to drop an entire percentage point. Such disregard for due dates sizzled the admin-drone's circuits. Surely the executor would want to know that the employee he intended to send on a priority one call was the same delinquent preventing his organization from achieving a one hundred percent compliance record.

"Statement: Is the executor aware that employee 1-X has not completed her annual training?"

"Where is she?"

The machine tilted it's optical receptor as it searched the personnel tracking logs. "Response: Last known location, server farms."

The Executor sat back in his chair. "Inform Dash that she needs to get her happy aft down to Dig Site four immediately."

"Follow-up: And the training slides?"

The businessman flicked his wrist dismissively. "Feel free to remind her when you get there."

MT-3R nodded its optical receptor. "Acknowledged." While automatons did not require such gestures for communication, studies showed that humans felt more comfortable around machines that mimicked their body movements. Therefore, the admin-drone incorporated human-like gestures into as many interactions as possible. As the hoverton spun around to leave, a jolt of energy surged through its circuits. Perhaps it could still achieve a ninety-seven percent compliance rating after all.

Chapter 4: Server Farms

After descending to the basement, MT-3R navigated to sublevel one, room 1-11, the server farms. When the machine passed through the doors, its audio receptors picked up a faint noise toward the back of the room. The hoverton fluttered through the rows of server racks, following its origin.

"Query: Employee 1-X, are you in here?" the admin-drone called out, amplifying its speaker output.

No response came.

MT-3R continued in the direction of the faint noise, weaving through the maze of machinery. As the automaton approached the back of the room, its optics glimpsed a cubical with an L-shaped workstation. A mountain of electronic components covered the surface. Coffee cups littered the remaining desk space. Rows of books filled the shelves but they weren't manuals, they were fiction. The titles varied in genre. Most were sword-and-sorcery fiction. MT-3R never understood why organics read such rubbish. It was illogical to read anything that didn't increase productivity. The very few non-fiction books on the shelf were gaming how-to guides and coding manuals. Above the books, a holo-frame displayed a wizard facing off against a dragon. On the other side of the table, a woman sat hunched over with her back to the hoverton.

"Statement: Employee 1-X, the Executor sent for you."

Again, the woman did not respond.

Was she okay?

MT-3R's phonic receptors indicated that the faint noise it had followed, seemed to emanate from the woman herself. It increased and dissipated with the rise and fall of the woman's chest. The sound resembled wheezing. The machine cocked it's metallic neck as it processed the information. Was the woman snoring?

The hoverton fluttered closer.

The woman startled awake, looking from side-to-side, her disheveled strawberry blonde hair concealed her face. "What's that ticking noise?"

"Response: Employee 1-X most likely is referring to this machine's faulty motivator. It is overdue for maintenance."

The server farmer stretched, then scratched the back of her neck. "Sounds like," she yawned, "a clock."

"Reminder: Sleeping on duty is against company policy."

Keeping her back to MT-3R, the woman picked up a piece of equipment and scanned it with her utility cuff. "So is scheduling employees for two double-shifts in a row. But the company doesn't seem to care about that, now do they?"

"Question: Employee 1-X, is your holocom broken?"

"Nope. I switched it off." She continued to perform diagnostics on the server components.

"Statement: 1-X, the Executor requires your assistance."

"Oh yeah?" The woman pressed a few buttons on the workstation keyboard. "Tell Buzz to blow it out his air-shaft. I'm busy here."

The hoverton fluttered backward. 1-X's suggestion did not compute. Protocols prohibited automatons from utilizing profanity with organics. An automaton manager should know this. Nevertheless, the topic of the executor appeared to agitate 1-X. According to conversation protocols, the most effective way to get someone to assist you was to build rapport, and the best way to do that was to engage them in small talk.

The machine knew exactly the subject to bring up.

"Reminder: Did 1-X know that annual training slides are due next week?"

The woman sighed. "I'm a little preoccupied." She gestured toward the rows of server racks. "Some sort of strange code is wreaking havoc on the ton-net. If we don't figure out what's causing it, every automaton in this colony could be affected."

"Continuation: Does 1-X realize that only one week remains to accomplish the training? As a team member, every individual's efforts—or lack thereof—reflect poorly on the organization."

The woman raised a finger. "So, what you're saying is, I still have seven more days to finish."

As MT-3R considered that path of logic, the woman paused. "Wait, Buzz sent you down here to remind me about training slides?"

"Statement: Negative. Dig Site Four issued a priority one request."

1-X waved her hand in dismissal. "Probably just another drill."

"Clarification: According to installation security chief, John Griff, salvagers are trapped in the tunnels, running out of air."

The woman swiveled her chair to face the machine.

Emerald eyes stared out through strawberry hair. Freckles covered her cheeks and a cybernetic implant etched the left side of the woman's face. The tattoo-like technology snaked down her neckline, all the way beneath the collar. In all of MT-3R's interactions with bio-sapiens, whether birth-born, clone, or refugee, the machine had never encountered such a marking.

"Additionally, 1-X has training slides due next week."

The woman raised a hand.

"Whoa, too fast, slow down."

The machine is titled it's metal neck piece. This did not compute. MT-3R had calibrated it's speech processor for optimal levels yesterday afternoon. Perhaps the woman was still groggy from her nap. The machine slowed its speech speed down by ten percent, then repeated itself, making an extra effort to articulate the words clearly. "Clarification: Security. Training. Slides. Are. Due. Next—"

"Wait, wait, wait," the woman said, furrowing her eyebrows.

MT-3R paused.

"First of all, enough with the 1-X business. Call me Dash. Second, what did the chief say? Salvagers are trapped in the tunnels?"

The machine nodded its optical receptor. "Affirmative. The slide screen will not activate."

Dash placed her holo-pad on the desk and stared at her utility cuff for a moment, "I wonder..." Her words trailed off. What did she wonder? MT-3R couldn't stand it when organics did this. How hard was it to finish a sentence? After another moment of rumination, the woman stood up and grabbed her company issued enviro-suit, then began to don the gear.

"Query: Is an enviro-suit necessary?"

The woman smirked as she continued to piece together the outfit. "A knight doesn't go into battle without their armor. It's the only way to stay safe."

"Confusion: This unit does not see the correlation."

Dash rolled her eyes, then placed the virtual vizard over her head like a hair band. "The company gave me a mask." She pressed a button and the visor dropped down covering her face, then the heads-up-display activated. "So I'm going to wear it." As she said the words, the helmet's built-in microphone augmented her voice. "Besides, it looks stellar and makes me sound all official."

Once she donned the rest of the gear, Dash faced MT-3R. "How do I look?"

"Response: Like a human."

The woman sighed audibly through her mask. "Listen," Dash said, examining the machine, "M.T.H.R., that's your designation, right? First off, when someone asks you how they look, always respond 'great.' Got it?"

"Acknowledged."

"Also, M.T.-3.R. isn't going to work for me. You need something catchy that highlights your personality." She stared at the ceiling for a moment, then snapped her fingers. "Mother. Yes, that's it. From now on, you'll respond to Mother."

The machine didn't know how to process this new directive. While its programming did not agree with the use of a moniker, for nicknames were inefficient and illogical, the woman had taken time out of her day to come up with something creative to call MT-3R. This suggested that the human cared about Mother, which also suggested that the machine's attempt to build rapport succeeded. Therefore if the admin-drone accepted this new directive, the probability the human would complete the annual training slides on time increased by five percent. But this minor success posed a greater problem. The hoverton never had a friend before. A thousand questions regarding human relationships flooded its processor in a microsecond. Were there protocols, timelines, quantifiable metrics?

As the machine explored the answers to these data points, Dash marched straight toward the exit. The hoverton fluttered about for a moment, not sure what to do next. Technically the machine had accomplished its task.

Dash turned to the hoverton. "Well sidekick, are you coming? Time to go be big blasted heroes."

Chapter 5: Does That Fall Under The Job Description?

By the time Dash had arrived, emergency teams had already flooded the area. Lights flashed and sirens blared, as response personnel and medi-tons swarmed the dig site. Dash could easily avoid Buzz if she blended in with the crowd.

Mother fluttered in front of her. "Statement: This unit has notified the executor of our arrival." Buzz stood along the outskirts sipping on another Astaro-cola. Swishing the slushy in his hands, he kept his eyes locked on Dash. *So much for flying under the radar.* "Stellar, thanks Mother." Dash strode past the machine, directly into the sea of automatons.

The executive followed.

"Perhaps we should start work tomorrow, once you're ready to answer the holocom?" Buzz said once he caught up to her.

"I was busy," Dash said, continuing toward the dig site entrance.

"Doing what exactly?"

"My job."

The executor cut in front of Dash, blocking her from going any further.

She placed her hands on her hips.

He pressed those stupid coke-bottle glasses to the bridge of his nose, then he just stood there in silence. If he thought she was going to give him the pleasure of a response, he had another thing coming. Dash had nothing to say to the brickhead.

Mother's optical receptor panned back and forth between the executive and the server technician several times. "Insight: This unit found Dash investigating anomalous code in the server farms."

Dash shot the hoverton laser eyes. Whose side was this blabber bot on anyways?

The executor raised an eyebrow. "Is that so?"

"Something's messing with the slave circuits on the ton-net. So I checked it out."

He waved a hand dismissively. "You're not in the military anymore. Investigation isn't part of the job description. You're just a simple server farmer."

Dash ignored the comment and sidestepped past him. *What a vac'n wormhole.*

"It would be so unfortunate if I had to mark you down on your next appraisal. Who knows how that could affect your application for transfer."

Dash spun around. "Stellar. So maybe *you* can fix that then?" She gestured toward the control panel. "It's not like *that's* in my job description either."

Mother fluttered next to the Executor. "Confirmation: Dash is correct. Extemporaneous tasks of this nature do not fall within a server technician's job description." The machine turned to Dash. "However, completing annual training slides is a requirement for all employees, and clearly spelled out in the contract Dash signed at time of employment."

Dash rolled her eyes. For a second there, she thought the bucket of bolts was actually going to strengthen her argument. She placed her hands on her hips. "Imagine an executive that did their own work. Wouldn't that be a sight."

Buzz stood silent, stirring his straw.

Dash shrugged, then headed toward the exit.

"Thank the stars, you're here." A big guy wearing colony-security armor waved a holopad, then hastened to Dash's side.

She paused. Was he talking to her?

The rotund officer turned to Buzz. "Is this your tech?"

The wormhole glanced at Dash, then nodded.

The gruff man held out his hand. "John Griff, chief security officer."

Dash stared at his hand. "What seems to be the problem, Chief?"

The chief pursed his lips, then dropped his hand back to his side. "We have some salvagers stuck down in the tunnels. The whole system is on lockdown and we can't get the slide screen to open."

"Have you tried troubleshooting the access panels?"

He handed her his holo-pad. "According to my men, they tried everything."

Dash pressed a few buttons, then reviewed the display. "So they attempted a hard reboot?"

The chief nodded. "Against my better judgment. Didn't fix a thing. Matter fact, we had to evacuate Dig Site Six."

The executor cocked an eyebrow. "Evacuate? Why?"

"Come to find out, both sites run on the same grid. So when we shut down Four, Six went too. Took out perimeter defenses for over an hour. They're back up now, but I didn't want to take any chances with pantras and Bush People roaming just outside the gate. Luckily, that facility is all but shut down, so only a few personnel were affected."

"Six was shut down?"

"Budget cuts. Don't get me started."

Buzz aimed his soft-drink at Dash. "Well it's a good thing I brought you our best technician."

Dash handed Chief Griff the holo-pad back, then glanced at Buzz. "The Executor exaggerates. I'm just a simple server farmer. And to be honest, I'm not even sure if this type of situation falls under *my* job description."

Buzz nearly choked on his drink, then tugged at his tie and cleared his throat.

Luckily her mask was tinted, so he couldn't see her smirking. *Serves you right, starweed.*

"Nonsense. You're already down here," Chief Griff said. "Give it a shot. I've already agreed to the Executor's terms."

"Supplemental Information: The employee is correct. This task does not fall within-"

Buzz raised a hand. "Thank you admin-drone. The chief is well aware. That will be all." He stared at Dash, "Whether you can fix the problem or not, just think of how this opportunity will affect company relations between colonists and contractors." His eyes widened. "And your next performance report."

She ignored the veiled threat and directed her attention to Griff. "I don't know if there's much more I can do if your people already attempted a hard boot."

The security chief placed his hand on Dash's shoulder. "Think of the workers trapped down there. Think of their wives and children. Let them go home to their families. Give them a chance to dream tonight."

She removed her cyber stylus and started toward the control panel. The motto of her military tech school echoed through her mind. A motto she had come to internalize over the years. "A wizard's job is never done."

Chapter 6: Trashtons And Green Glyphs

Fantasies can be categorized into three types. The first kind is a general fantasy. They entail your aspirations, goals, and future plans. These are the things you tend to share with your friends, family, and colleagues. If you asked Dash, those were the blandest and most superficial of the three types. The second kind are far more exciting because they give you a secret glimpse into a person's wild side. They're all the spicy intimacies that people imagine when no one else is around. If you're lucky, you get to share these desires with a spouse or lover. Despite their devilish details, you and your darling can delight in their delectable decadence for days on end. But then there's the third type of fantasy; the kind that's so dark you couldn't possibly tell anyone else, lest you risk getting in trouble. They're so bad, that sometimes you feel guilty that you even allowed your mind to think them. Sometimes... But today, today Dash didn't feel bad at all. As she approached the portal mainframe, she relished in the third type of fantasy. She daydreamed about all of the ways Buzz might meet an untimely demise. Most of them involved him choking on his soda straw.

Raindrops trickled between the crevices of her enviro-suit as Dash opened up the portal's control panel. Why was it always so blasted dreary on this planet? Flash storms and constant fog did not make it on the list of Dash's favorite weather ever. And why was she outside in the first place? She was a server farmer for star's sake.

Whatever.

She didn't care. Just as long as she was as far away from Buzz as possible. What a wormhole. How could anyone in upper management think he was qualified for a leadership position? The man knew nothing about the actual job and cared little for the people who did. Not just Dash. Buzz was like that with everyone. The company man treated all employees as if *they* were automatons; expendable resources that could be replaced by simply buying new ones.

Once she removed the casing, she pressed a button on the control panel and a holo-display blossomed from the machine. Dash unclipped the cyber-stylus from her utility cuff, then scanned the information. The device ran diagnostic tests and transmitted them to her virtual vizard's heads-up display. Various error messages bombarded the screen. According to system logs, a waste management ton went outside of its designated route and triggered an unauthorized access alarm, which in turn prevented the slip-drive from activating.

What in the Twelve Realms would cause a trash-ton to stray off its predesignated path?

Ring. Ring.

Her utility cuff indicated an incoming call from Avalon Del Cutter. Dash answered it. "Hey, I'm a little busy right now. Can I call you back?"

"Really quick, just wanted to make sure you were still good to watch Astrea tomorrow."

Dash squinted. "Tomorrow?"

"Dash, the *thing*."

"The thing..."

"The thing. *Tomorrow*. Don't tell me you forgot."

"No, no. I didn't forget." In reality, Dash had no clue as to which 'thing' her best friend was referencing. With Avalon, it was always something.

"Oh thank the stars. The nannytons were all booked. So, is it cool if I drop her off tomorrow morning?"

"Tomorrow morning... of course. I'm sure we can find something to do."

"Stellar! Dash, you're the best. What would I do without you?"

"I don't know. Save money. Stay at home. Learn how to cook."

Avalon laughed. "Never!"

"Okay, got it. Tomorrow. The thing. I'm watching Astrea." Dash shook her head as she ended the call. *Typical Avalon.*

She returned her attention back to the control panel and punched in the system override, attempting to reactivate the portal.

The panel beeped in error.

She tried to reset the system.

The panel beeped at her again.

"Well, it was worth a try."

"Query: Has Dash identified the problem?"

The admin-drone hovered beside her. Dash had forgotten that the hoverton was even there. Apparently the flying frisbee thought they were best friends now. Dash sighed inwardly. *Automatons.* Every day the brainless blockheads flooded her office with problems. Poor excuses for workers, if you asked her.

Faulty logic. Corrupted thought processes. Wrong pathways. Automatons couldn't function without someone guiding them. They needed constant instruction; someone telling them exactly what to do and when to do it. If one directive wasn't clear, it could bring an entire project to a halt.

"Looks like a trash-ton caused this mess. I'll have to sift through some files to clear this up."

After pressing a few buttons on her utility cuff, the system's internal codes cascaded down the holo-display. The enviro-mask HUD scanned the stream of information. Nothing seemed out of the ordinary.

Sun spit.

Why couldn't anything just be straight forward?

Dash tapped the cyber stylus on the control panel. Something must be preventing the slide screen from connecting.

Droplets beaded on Dash's virtual vizard, obstructing her vision. She pressed a button on the side of the mask and the visor raised. Then she removed a cloth from her cargo pocket and wiped off the screen. *This mucking planet.* Her job was supposed to be inside working on server-

Wait, what was that?

An exotic symbol hovered over one of the files.

Where did that come from?

It looked like some sort of glyph, similar to the markings etched in the ruins.

Dash lowered her visor. The image disappeared.

Wait. What?

She raised her visor again. The symbol reappeared.

"Mother, can you detect anything out of the ordinary in this directory?" Dash pointed at the mysterious symbol.

The automaton craned its metal neck, then focused its cycloptic eye. "Negative."

"You don't see that green glyph, right there?"

The hoverton fluttered backward. "Confusion: This unit's optical receptors only detect system files emanating from the control panel."

Dash leaned in. Something in the code was preventing this anomaly from appearing on the digital scanners.

Fascinating.

She opened the holo-file and investigated. More exotic symbols appeared. The glyphs didn't resemble any language she'd ever seen before. The code manifested like a weed, planting seeds throughout the digital terrain. It cracked through the system safeguards like roots through concrete. Without directed pathways, the programs were free to go any which way they pleased. "Mother, analyze the activity logs," Dash said, grabbing a holo-brick of anomalous code and tossing it in the machine's direction. "Try to find out when this code was introduced into the system."

The hoverton complied. "Query: Has Dash found something?"

"Looks like we're dealing with a virus."

Mother scanned the holo-brick with its cycloptic red eye. "Analysis: Records indicate this code entered the system at the same time that the waste management automaton entered the building."

"Where is the trash-ton assigned?"

"Response: Dig Site six."

"Near the Crimson Forest?"

"Affirmative."

Interesting.

The servers Dash was working on earlier oversaw that same dig site. Perhaps there was a connection between the anomalies in the servers and this code? She glanced at the watch on her utility cuff.

"I'll have to look into that later."

Dash scanned the rest of the code with her cyber-stylus.

"Good news. It seems to be contained within this program directory."

From what she saw, the virus hadn't spread beyond the local folder. The salvage-ton programs and other system critical folders didn't appear to be affected. That was lucky. Buzz would have a conniption if any automatons had to be taken off-line. Nevertheless, she wanted to run a full scan of this anomalous code once they got back. That, and the trash-ton.

"Need a backdoor into the system. But first, I'm going to take a few samples of this code."

She ran the cyber-stylus across the code. The device scanned the string of symbols and saved them to a containment disk. Once she finished copying the code, she clipped the cyber-stylus back into its compartment.

Now, how to break into the system? According to Chief Griff the techtons already followed the normal protocol, even performing a hard boot. So, nothing orthodox would work. No. She'd have to get creative.

Dash removed the uplink cord from the mainframe and connected it to her virtual vizard. "I'm going to have to plug in and get a closer look." If her years in the military working as a wizard taught her anything, it was that sometimes, you just had to look beyond the textbook answer and see things from a different perspective.

The machine nodded it's cycloptic eye, "Acknowledged."

Dash pressed a few buttons on her utility cuff, activating the connection with the mainframe. Her HUD switched to black, then repopulated the screen with an overlay. First a blue sky filled with blocky clouds appeared. Then green grass. Next, rudimentary shapes like cubes, spheres, and pyramids populated the digital environment. Some were trees, some were structures, and others were roads. This was a virtual representation of the digsite master program list. To Dash, it resembled a small town. Larger buildings represented program folders, while smaller items represented files. Next her avatar appeared. She thought it looked like a 3-D version of a poorly drawn stick figure that needed to go on a diet. She sighed. The graphics were a far cry from most modern plug cartridges. But what could you expect from a government funded facility? Still, while it wasn't *Sins of the Serpent,* Dash enjoyed working in basic environments like this. They were clean, simple, and easy to navigate.

She awkwardly marched her block person into town.

The scene before her was utter chaos.

Security programs ran rampant along the digital landscape. Rather than following pre-designated tasks, they seemed to be working on their own accord, outside of the guidelines set by the governing program. Almost like an artificial intelligence or a virtual intelligence. *But that's not possible.* Not only did laws prohibit such behavior, company code was specifically written to prevent the digital puppets from thinking for themselves.

Dash followed the anomalous activity to its origin. It led her avatar to a small structure in the center of the town. Giant olive-colored vines snaked along the brick-colored surface. According to the sign above the entrance this building represented a subprogram folder. Dash went inside to examine the underlying files and couldn't believe her eyes. The room resembled a scene from a post-apocalyptic story. Weeds filled the room. But, rather than a 16-bit display, they were rendered in high definition. Each one streamed a code with more exotic glyphs like the one she'd seen just moments ago.

What in the Twelve Realms was going on?

Dash reviewed the files. *That's not good.* The anomalous code had already infected several of the dig site's security protocols. She'd have to quarantine the building quickly, before the virus could spread. Dash raised her enviromask.

"First, we need to neutralize the code, then we can reset the system." She pressed a few buttons on her utility cuff and a list of her personal folders appeared on the holo-display. She clicked on the one named "spells."

"Query: How exactly will you create a backdoor?"

Dash scrolled through the list of folders. "Simple. I'll cast a spell."

"Confusion: This unit can only assume your statement is figurative in nature, yet Mother cannot understand the metaphorical significance."

"When I served in the Crypto Force, they taught us that working with code is like dealing with magic. As a matter of fact, my O.M.S.D was 'cryptologic wizard.'"

"Query: What does O.M.S.D stand for?"

"Official military specialty designator," Dash said, pressing a few buttons on her utility cuff.

The ton fell silent, apparently processing that new piece of information.

"Now, that virus is like some sort of black magic, corrupting everything it touches. I'm going to use white magic to get rid of it."

"Magic?" the admin-drone said, incredulously.

"Mother, don't be such a ton."

"Confusion: Mother has no choice but to be an automaton. Its programming doesn't permit it to be anything else."

Dash rolled her eyes. "Never mind. Just forget the whole magic analogy." She scrolled to the spell folder called *destruction* and selected a program named *viriditas exitium*. She removed a holo-brick of the code. "This is a personal favorite of mine. Cooked it up myself."

"Query: What is it?"

"Basically a weed eater. Should get rid of the virus, and give us back control." Dash took a holo-brick of the contaminated code and held it up. "Essentially, this virus is like a weed. It's breaking through the system and preventing company protocols from maintaining control." In her other hand, she held a holo-brick of the spell-code. "This spell summons a program that behaves like a hound dog. It will hunt down any code I designate." Dash combined the two holo-bricks and they merged into one. "I just gave it the virus' scent. Now, I introduce it into the system." She entered the combined holo-brick into the interface. Lines of code cascaded across the holo-display, as paragraphs of information disappeared. "Then it hunts down the virus, and destroys it."

After a few more moments the system recycled and came back online.

"Alakazam." She clapped her hands, then fluttered her fingers. "It's gone. Just like magic." She typed in the command to open the dig site portal, then raised her hand in the air, like a wizard casting a spell. "Now, open sesame," she said, flourishing her finger to press the enter button.

The interface rang a confirmation sound and, from her periphery, Dash could see the slide screen connect and the portal materialize.

"Statement: Sensors indicate that all tunnel doors have opened."

"There you have it." Dash bowed, "Magic."

As she put away her tools, new questions formed in her mind. What was the mysterious code, and how in Quietus did it get through all of the company's safeguards? Could it be some sort of malicious code? If so, who used such exotic symbols?

Her mind jumped to the worst possible answer and a chill went down her spine.

No.

No.

That couldn't be possible. Could it?

Chapter 7: A Wizard's Job Is Never Done

It's not that Dash wanted to be fired. To the contrary, she quite enjoyed her mundane life here on Hestia. Nothing exciting ever happened at the Cube—well aside from today's incident. The basement was a quiet place where she was left to her own devices. Most of the colonists and clones were simple people and the tons were... Well, tons. Granted the dating pool was a bit dry. But for the most part that kept her from getting involved in messy entanglements. All and all, this was just the kind of job she'd always wanted. Safe and secure. But whenever Buzz got involved, she always ended up riding the snarky train into the station. She really couldn't help it. He just knew how to throttle her engines.

As Dash shut down the interface, she could hear cheers from the personnel behind her. She cringed. Dash wasn't one for big crowds. After finishing up at the control panel, she lowered her virtual vizard and examined the sea of people. Several salvagers trudged out of the tunnels, visibly exhausted. Medical teams rushed to check their vitals and hand out food and water. Perhaps she could sneak out without Buzz noticing. If the executor knew where she was heading, he would almost definitely disapprove. The wormhole stood next to another employee, sipping on what appeared to be yet another soft drink. Now was her chance. She turned to the admin-drone. "Mother, go inform the executor that everything is finished here."

"Acknowledged." The hoverton spun around and fluttered toward the executor.

Perfect.

She weaved through the sea of response personnel, keeping to the edge of the crowd.

Ring. Ring.

Her utility cuff indicated an incoming call from Avalon Del Cutter. Dash answered it. "Hey, I'm a little busy right now. Can I call you back?"

"Really quick, just wanted to make sure you were still good to watch Astrea tomorrow."

Dash squinted. "Tomorrow?"

"Dash, the *thing.*

"The thing..."

"The thing. *Tomorrow.* Don't tell me you forgot."

"No, no. I didn't forget." In reality, Dash had no clue as to which 'thing' her best friend was referencing. With Avalon, it was always something.

"Oh thank the stars. The nannytons were all booked. So, is it cool if I drop her off tomorrow morning?"

"Tomorrow morning... of course. I'm sure we can find something to do."

"Stellar! Dash, you're the best. What would I do without you?"

"I don't know. Save money. Stay at home. Learn how to cook."

Avalon laughed. "Never!"

"Okay, got it. Tomorrow. The thing. I'm watching Astrea." Dash shook her head as she ended the call. *Typical Avalon.*

From the corner of her eye Dash noticed a husky man heading toward her. Griff, the Chief Security Officer. So much for being inconspicuous.

"That was incredible. The tons worked for hours and couldn't do a damn thing. What's your name, young lady?" He extended his hand for a handshake.

Dash hesitated. The burly man snatched her hand before she could think of an excuse not to shake it. His firm grip nearly crushed her palm.

"Dash," she replied through gritted teeth.

"The medical team reported no casualties. They say the salvagers will be just fine."

He released her hand.

Dash shook it out, then massaged it. "Good to hear."

"Someone with your talents shouldn't be wasting away as a Cube technician."

She shrugged. "It's steady work and the pay is decent."

He nodded.

"You know, the job's done. You can take your vizard off now."

Dash inched back. She knew Griff meant well, but she didn't like removing her mask at work. "I'm uh..." she activated her utility cuff, "...still reviewing—"

"See, I told you. Our best technician. Worth every penny." Buzz interrupted. He slurped on an Astaro-Cola as he approached. The hoverton fluttered beside him. *Buzz was such a ton.* But since the chief was already here, maybe she could take advantage of the moment and use him as leverage.

She faced Griff.

"Chief, this incident was caused by a virus."

The security officer glanced at Buzz. "A virus?"

"Highly sophisticated. I've never seen anything like it before. It appears to be contained to a subset of folders. But I'd like to investigate a bit further. Seems to have originated from a malfunctioning trash-ton. The logs say that the ton came from Dig Site Six earlier this morning. If you don't mind, I'd like to take the machine offline and run some tests."

The chief nodded.

Dash glanced at Buzz, "And tomorrow I'd like to go to Six and examine those servers."

The executor gave her laser eyes.

The security chief shrugged. "Sounds good. I'll—"

One of his deputies cut in. "Chief, we got a bit of a problem."

"What is it, this time?"

"The Director requested a status report on the incident."

"How did *he* catch wind of this so quickly?"

The man shrugged. "My guess would be that Council rep, Dr. Nightingale."

Griff cursed under his breath, then turned to Dash and released a heavy sigh. "The fun never ends here." The security chief handed her his holopad. "Whatever you need, just make sure this event is contained. We don't want another lockdown. Especially with a UPC representative on planet. But be careful. Like I said, Six has become a bit of a ghost town ever since the wigs cut back our funding." He glanced over his shoulder. "Now, if you'll excuse me, I have to go explain all of this to the Director."

Dash nodded and took the holopad, then Chief Griff left.

Buzz skulked toward her, sifting his drink and glaring at her. "Dash, the consummate hero."

Dash ignored the comment and tucked the holopad under her arm. "I think that virus may be connected to the anomalies I found in the server farm. Tomorrow, I'm going to Dig Site Six to check it out."

Buzz shook his head. "You will do no such thing."

"But you heard Chief—"

He held up a hand. "This falls outside the scope of our contract. If the colonists want us to investigate further then they'll need to renegotiate the terms."

Dash raised her visor. "Buzz, this is more than just an automaton malfunction. I'm not sure if this is anomalous activity or industrial espionage. But lives are at stake, including yours." Dash leaned in and lowered her voice. "I think somebody may have introduced malicious code into our system."

The Executor scoffed. "For what purpose? To steal a bunch of ancient rocks? There's nothing of value on this planet."

Dash put her hands on her hips. "Maybe not, but you saw what happened today. Could you imagine if one of the main facilities went on lockdown? Or worse, headquarters?"

Buzz narrowed his eyes but did not respond. Instead, he stirred the straw of his drink.

She gestured toward the crowd of people beside them. "This is a security matter that involves the whole colony. We are required by law to investigate."

Buzz paused. No doubt he was calculating a way to twist some obscure policy into his argument. "Fine." He nodded at the hoverton. "The admin-drone will accompany you."

Dash and Mother faced each other.

The machine tilted its camcorder-shaped face. "Query: Does the executor wish for this unit to ensure that Dash completes the annual training slides?"

Buzz pointed his drink at Dash. "You will track her billable hours." Despite his skulking figure, the man's chest seemed to puff out slightly.

"Acknowledged," Mother focused its red optical lens on Dash. "There is always time for one more task."

"I'm fully capable of tracking my own hours, thank you very much."

"You're also fully capable of answering your holo-com, right?"

Dash pursed her lips. Several retorts came to mind, but none that she dared to say out loud.

He gestured at the admin-drone, "The ton goes with you."

Sun spit. What a snot sniffing, machine mucking, aft shaft.

Buzz pushed his coke-bottle glasses back to the top of his beak and took another sip from his straw.

How did she end up with this wormhole for a supervisor? Dash imagined shoving the drink directly down his gangly throat. She didn't have to put up with this. She was the top technician in the company. "You know, I heard that Excelsior doesn't even track hours. They pay their employees based on performance. I wonder what that's like?"

"Well, that's funny because I didn't think they hired people with your type of," he paused, "background." But who knows, maybe they'd make an exception in your case?"

My background? Vac' you Buzznard.

Why couldn't he get locked down in the mucking tunnels? Or eaten by a pantra? She frowned. As much as she hated to admit it, the executor was right. Dash couldn't quit. Dath Corp was the only business in the quadrant that would hire someone with a past like hers. Dash gave a pursed smile then marched toward the exit.

Chapter 8: Enter The Interverse

Arriving home after a double shift was always a good feeling. Except when a smelly trash-ton is sitting at your doorstep.

That evening when Dash returned to her trailer, she found a cargo bin sitting at her doorstep. Inside of it sat the trashton that had caused the lockdown. After removing her mask, she examined the machine. Rust stripes tarnished its chassis. "You look like you just came out of the cyberwars." She crinkled her nose. "And smell like it too." Dash wheeled the robot inside, then took it to her personal workstation and hooked it up.

She pressed a few buttons on the holo-interface, instructing the system to clean the trashton. Honestly, she needed a shower to0. While she waited for the cleanser pool to boot, she rubbed her hands together. They always kept it so cold inside this blasted place. Many clones joked that the facility should be renamed the Ice Cube, and she agreed.

Beep.

Click.

Whir.

The system lit up and the program activated. The platform lowered, dipping the trashton into a cleansing bath. "I'll deal with *you* tomorrow."

Dash removed a dirty dish from the couch, then plopped down. She grabbed one of the recreational plugs from the coffee table and inserted it into the uplink vein in her forearm. Next she connected the other end of the cord to her neural headset and donned the goggle-looking gaming device. A virtual reality displayed before her eyes. Unlike the blocky graphics from the outdated plug at the digsite, this next-gen device generated in ultra definition. And the neuroleptics it secreted were stellar. Every muscle in her body relaxed as the sedative set in. The feeling was euphoric.

Her avatar loaded and she found herself in *The Market,* which was basically the digital equivalent of a megamall for video games. Players from across the interverse could log-in and interact with each other here. Some chatted. Some traded. Others came for... entertainment. A scantily dressed female avatar caught Dash's attention. The woman belly-danced atop a stage, while a patron ogled her figure, tossing bit-creds every time she flourished her aft in his face. Dash shook her head. For all anyone knew, the dancer could be a greasy old man in real life. Contrastingly it was possible that the patron might be a young kid. But how could anyone ever know for sure? That was both the upside and the downside of plugging. Anonymity. In the interverse, you could be anyone. You could do anything. The interverse was a place where you could act out your wildest dreams, your freakiest fantasies, or your darkest desires, and no one could ever judge you.

For Dash, it was an escape from the outside world. Here, she didn't have to hide behind a work mask or business attire. Here she could just be herself.

Now, fully integrated in the digital world, Dash could use her mind to control her avatar's movements. She walked past several shops waiting for her dashboard interface to populate. Some peddlers offered weapon enhancements, others potions and buffs, while even others offered new vehicles and mounts. At the far end of the mall walkway, she scoped the adventure she was looking for. *Dragon's Keep.* The entrance resembled the jaws of a monster. Snarled lips revealed sharp fangs. Glowing red eyes glared back at passers-by. Flashing lights above the monster's brow read *The Ultimate Journey.* According to her home-screen, most of her friends were already in the game, playing raid missions for the *Sins of the Serpent campaign.* She passed through the door and her avatar teleported to a loadout selection screen.

"Well look who decided to show up," a nasal voice said through her headset.

She rolled her eyes. "Save it Dell."

"What's the point of having a raid party, if no one shows up for the raid?" This time it was Tavin who complained.

She scrolled through her various presets until she arrived at her mage configuration. She selected it, then mystical artifacts and robes appeared on her avatar. "I had work."

"Well, I hope it was worth it. We've been getting crushed out here with no magic support."

Dash selected her legendary staff, *Archangel's Bane*, and stepped through the spawn point. Her avatar dematerialized, then reappeared at the front of a forest. The game's cinematic camera swept above the trees toward the mountain range beyond, then flew up the center of the summit, where a giant, silver-scaled dragon roared. Lighting struck and thunder boomed, while flying serpents kept watch in the clouds above. Then a narrator's voice said, "Welcome to Dragon's Keep."

"A wizard's job is never done," Dash said, then she joined her party at the edge of the treeline. They were fighting a pack of drats. Her friends were making quick work of the rat-sized dragon creatures. This was the typical start of a campaign. Dash knew that the tiny foes represented a smaller version of the larger boss they would end up fighting later in the game. These low level monsters gave players an idea of what type of fighting strategies would work against the larger opponents. Since they were facing drats, that meant the final boss would be a dragon of some sort. Most likely a storm dragon considering the opening scene of the campaign.

Dell's ranger stood in the middle of the drat pack, flinging the wretched beasts off of his character and cutting them down with his strider sword. Meanwhile, Tavin used his archer to pick off the cretins with fire arrows. Dash sighed. At this pace, they wouldn't even make it to stage two. Everyone knew that storm dragons, even the smaller ones, have a high immunity to fire based weapons. Which resulted in the attacks having little debuff damage. Dash raised her avatar's hand to the sky and chanted a spell, then pointed her staff at the pack of drats. Each of the mongrel's contorted, then collapsed to the ground, bodies glowing blue-ish. The remains dissolved into energy orbs which were absorbed by Dash's cross-tipped staff.

"Come on. Shape it up, you guys."

Tavin's archer turned to Dash. "You know, we had that perfectly under control."

She grinned. "Yup. Another hour and maybe you would have cleared stage one." She turned to Dell and nodded, "What's up my ranger."

His avatar frowned. "Late as usual."

"Don't be jealous just because Dash is a big-time contractor now."

Wait, that voice, was that Gibs?

"Hyong Gibs is that you?"

A brawny male avatar adorned in Astral-knight armor, strode toward the team. "In the flesh," he said resting his obsidian longsword atop his shoulder. "Well, sort of."

"Gibs, hey! I didn't know you were back."

Their avatars exchanged a wingman handshake, clasping around the thumbs, then pulling each other in for a half hug, half chest bump.

"Just got in."

"I thought plugging was frowned upon for you big-wig, upper management types?"

The astral knight placed a finger to his lips. "First of all, I'm not a wig. Second, this will be our little secret. So, what had you tied up anyway?"

"Had a situation at one of the digsites today. Whole thing went on lockdown and the tons couldn't get it open."

"Sounds serious."

"Nah," She waved her hand. "I took care of it. But oh man, Gibs, you should have seen the look on Buzznard's face. The wormhole was so furious, that he threatened to block my transfer request."

"Got to take it easy there champ. You may be the snappiest coder in the quadrant. But those mid-management policy pushers have frail egos. All they care about is numbers and the bottom line. If you're not careful, you'll end up working the server farms for the rest of your career."

"Wow, Gibsy. Do you hear yourself? You've been climbing up the company ladder so fast, you're starting to sound just like them; telling people what to do. That high life is making you soft."

He chuckled.

Dell, stepped in between them. "Can we focus here?"

"Yeah, it's almost supper time," Tavin chimed in.

Gibs bowed. "Lead the way, beautiful maiden."

Dash smirked. Tavin's archer was a slender, light-skinned she-elf with golden blonde hair—wearing the skimpiest of outfits—which was completely absurd, because that was the exact opposite of how *he* looked in real life.

Tavin seductively gestured down the rocky path. "This way me lords."

Dell's character elbowed past the three of them and started toward the woods. "I'm the ranger. I will lead the party, thank you very much." Tavin shrugged and followed suit. Gibs made an exaggerated face and mimed his hand so it looked like Dell complaining. Dash giggled, then they joined in after them. The team trekked through the brush and foliage till they came across a dirt path.

"I'm hungry. Are you guys hungry?"

"Tavin, you're always hungry."

"Quiet down." Dell said.

Gibs turned to Dash. "So, the digsite went on lockdown? How does something like that even happen?"

"I have my suspicions."

"Okay, that sounds ominous."

"What if we took a five-minute snack break before we get to the next waypoint?" Tavin interjected.

"We are not taking a snack break. We just got started," Dell responded.

Gibs ignored them both and looked back to Dash. He obviously wanted an answer.

Dash had intentionally given a vague response. She wasn't sure how much she should say about the incident. First off, she didn't want to alarm her friends. Plus, she wasn't sure how secure their current connection was. Not to mention, she could be wrong. It could have just all been a coincidence. But she knew Gibs. Her friend wouldn't let it go until she gave him something solid.

"Remember Kosan?"

"You mean the worst assignment in the Twelve Realms. Yeah, why?"

"We're going to agro every monster in this place, if you three don't quiet down." Dell whispered over his shoulder.

"The code was similar to that."

Gibs turned and gave Dash a knowing glance.

"Oh man," Tavin said. "That's not-"

Thwack.

His she-elf bumped into Dell. The ranger avatar held up his hand, signaling the group to halt.

The team stopped.

Dell gave Tavin laser eyes, then gesticulated with his fingers to look ahead.

The path ended at a stream, and a rickety bridge connected the edge of the forest with the foot of the mountain. They had reached the threshold. But that wasn't all. Something moved in the distance.

Something big.

Dell knelt down, picked up a stick, and wrote in the sand.

River troll.

Troll's were larger than humanoids but smaller than dragons. They weren't the hardest opponent in the game. But they were strong enough to take out the whole team if you weren't careful.

Tavin snatched the stick from Dell, then wrote his own message.

Snack break.

Gibs stepped between them and erased the words with his boot. Next, he unsheathed a dagger from his belt and sketched an attack plan, pointing to each member of the team when it was their part. Basically, he would act as the tank, attracting the monster's attention. Tavin and Dell would provide cover fire, and Dash would use healing buffs to keep the team alive.

"Bad idea," Dell whispered. "There could be more of them. We need to sneak around this area and swim across the stream."

"Are you kidding me? That will take too long. I want to eat now," Tavin snorted.

"Dell, I have work tomorrow. So we either take this thing down now or I'm plugging off," Gibs said.

The ranger frowned. "But we haven't even gotten to the mountain drakes yet."

Dell looked to Dash for support.

She placed a hand on his shoulder. "Sorry, my ranger. I've got stuff tomorrow too."

Tavin's character notched an arrow onto her bow. "Looks like the vote for a snack break passes, three to one."

Dell clasped his strider sword. "This is a bad idea."

Gibs tilted his head. "That's what makes it so much fun," he said, then charged the monster head-on. The creature bellowed an alarm and two more trolls rushed in. Dell raced to Gibs's aid, while Dash and Tavin provided support from the rear. But it wasn't enough. Within a matter of minutes, the trolls had defeated the whole team.

Their characters respawned at the last autosave point, near the beginning of the dirt trail.

"Well that went well," Dash said.

Dell threw his hands up in the air. "No one ever listens to me. We should have snuck around them."

"Yeah, but that was way more fun," Gibs said.

Tavin raised a finger. "At least we can get some food now. Meet back here tomorrow, same time?"

"How about on time?" Dell said.

Dash sighed. "Yes, yes. I really want to get to the dragon, so we can get that loot. Tomorrow night is *the* night." Everyone nodded in agreement. After that, Tavin logged off and Dell switched to a different game, leaving Dash and Gibs in the forest.

Dash fist-bumped the astral knight's breastplate. "It was good seeing you Gibs.

He placed a hand on her shoulder. "I miss you champ."

"Yeah, well things haven't been the same since you left. Everything is so quiet."

"If you two are going to catch up, switch to a private chat. Some of us are actually playing tonight," Dell complained.

They both smirked at each other, then complied with their friend's request.

Gibs's knight paused and looked her straight in the eye. "I didn't plug in just to play tonight." His avatar's expression was solemn. "I shouldn't tell you this, but you're the only one I can trust." He looked down at his feet, "I may never come back, and I just want someone to know."

"What are you talking about?"

Gib's avatar glanced around the area, then leaned in. "I made some friends at this last assignment," he said in a whisper. "We're going to pull our resources together and start a personal security business."

"You're starting your own company?" Dash asked, incredulous.

"Quiet." He looked about. "You've got a mouth louder than an exhaust port."

Dash ducked down. "Okay. Okay. I'm quiet. See. We're on private chat anyways. No one can hear me."

"I have a friend that knows a guy that made big money on investments in Worsteen. He's already got a couple of gigs lined up for us."

Dash shook her head. "Guns for hire? Doesn't that seem a little crazy? I mean, what happens if you end up losing everything? You've worked so hard to get where you are. They're planning on making you a prime soon. You'll be a bonafide wig."

Gibs stood up straight. "I know it's a risk. But if it doesn't work out, I'll do what I can on my own." He grabbed her arm. "It's what we've always talked about Dash."

Dash pursed her lips.

"I'm not going to wait around for the conglomerate to downsize and force me into retirement. Opportunities are spreading throughout the galaxy like starfire, and I want to take advantage of them before my model becomes outdated and gets replaced."

Dash shrugged him off. "Yeah. Meanwhile, I'm stuck here in the aft-end of space."

"You'll get your chance to transfer out. You're going to Atlantopolis next cycle, right?"

"Not likely. I may need to cancel the application."

"Wait. What for?"

"The office down here is undermanned."

Gibs sighed. "Really?"

"I'm serious. The Bush People are getting worse. I heard they even raided the shuttle-mart last month."

"Come on Dash. Chief Griff could fend off a whole army of Bush People with a single pulsar rifle."

"I know. But Soren assured me that they have almost secured enough server farms to run remote operations. Once they're set, I'll get my transfer. He just needs me to stay on for one more cycle."

"Soren? Look, I know you're close with the general. But he doesn't know everything. At some point, you're going to have to start making your own decisions."

"He's like a father to me."

"I know the old man's been there for you. But what good is all that work you're doing if the conglomerate just takes credit for it anyway? Did you hear that they plan on removing patent claims in the upcoming vote? Won't be long till you and those colonists are just a bunch of slaves, working for their conglomerate task-masters."

"Gibs, you know that wouldn't happen here. How many times have you said it yourself? The conglomeration doesn't care about a trash planet like this. Center Space is where all of the money's at. We're in the Frontier for star's sake."

Gib's avatar reflected an undeniably disappointed expression.

Dash paused. "But I do wish I was going with you."

"Well, we could always use a coder with your expertise." He seemed to force a smile. "Maybe someday." She could hear the disappointment in his voice

"Yeah," Dash said enthusiastically. "I'll transfer to Atlantopolis next cycle, then who knows." Despite how much she hoped that was true, her words didn't even sound convincing to herself.

Gibs's avatar held a concerned expression.

"Don't worry, I won't let them suck me into some 20-year contract of indentured servitude." She held out her hand.

They exchanged another wingman handshake.

"When your company makes it big, just remember who your best friend was."

"I will," Gibs said. "Take it easy, champ." Then he logged off.

Chapter 9: Dig Site Six

B*eep.*
Beep.

Beep.

Dash woke up to her alarm clock blaring.

Was it morning already?

She stretched, then sat up and turned off the device. The aroma of caffeine-filled her nostrils. Ah yes, the elixir of the gods. Just what she needed to wake up. Thank the stars for coffee machines with preset timers. Chatter came from outside. Dash peered out from the blinds of her trailer window. Outside, a team of class-twos marched toward the hover-bus station, no doubt ready for their workday. Some men, some women. It was easy to spot clones by their outfits. While each of them had a different hairstyle and personality, they all dressed the same, walked the same, and talked the same. They all fit in. Not like Dash. She didn't fit in anywhere. Not with emulations, not with colonists, not even with the refugees. Dash shook her head. "No thank you." Not only was she more effective on her own, but the machines were easier to get along with. They followed simple, predictable patterns. And best of all, they didn't judge. She released her finger from the blinds and they snapped back in place.

Dash hobbled to the kitchen and poured some coffee into her mug, then added a generous helping of creamer. She glanced at the holocard above her sink. The photo depicted sandy shores reaching out toward a deep blue ocean. In the distance, sun rays peeked out from behind the Atlantopolis pyramids. The caption read, New Egypt Awaits. She smiled and held the cup in her palms. The warm surface thawed out her fingers.

As she sipped the blonde roast, Dash scrolled through her holo-feed. Quadrant headlines populated the Dashboard. Conglomerate stocks were at an all-time high. Politicians from Center Space passed a bill that would allow more refugee owned and operated businesses to apply for government contracts. Religious zealots protested against references to Daynanic deities in the public-school curriculum, and new environmental studies claimed that portal travel could have adverse effects on the galacta-spiral winds. She shook her head and checked on the weather. According to the radar models, a major storm front was expected to push through later this afternoon. Dash cocked an eyebrow. If she wanted time to investigate Dig Site Six, she would have to leave soon.

She sighed, turning her attention to the cleansing station, where the trashton sat slumped over like a withering plant. She'd have to analyze it later. Today she was going to figure out what was going on at Dig Site Six. But the thought of being somewhere other than her workstation bothered her.

Somewhere with no walls.

Somewhere with no air conditioning.

Somewhere with no coffee. Blegh!

But at least in the meantime, the system could run a diagnostic check on the trashton while she was out. She transferred the ton to her private workstation and plugged in a few wires, then she activated the holo-display and pressed a few buttons. The diagnostic program started to run. Columns of code rained over the screen. She took another sip of coffee, then donned her envirosuit. Hopefully, the computer would have answers for her when she got back.

Knock. Knock. Knock.

Someone was at the door.

"Who in the realms..." Dash said, peeking through the peephole. Dash's eyes went wide. Avalon and Astrea stood outside. She had totally forgotten about babysitting today. "One second."

Dash opened the door.

Astrea raced inside and hugged Dash's leg, almost knocking her over.

Her mother handed Dash a backsack, "I'm actually running late. All of her stuff's in here."

Dash took the bag. "Av, how long is this thing of yours going to take?"

"Probably all day. Is that cool?"

"Yeah, I just have to take care of some work today." Dash figured it wouldn't hurt to bring the kid along.

"Look what I got Miss Dash." A hoverball floated in the air above the child. Astrea used her utility cuff to direct the golden orb.

"Got it for her file-day," Avalon said, reapplying a fresh coat of lipstick.

"That's so super-sonic," Dash said, ruffling the child's hair. "My sisters and I had one of those when we were little."

Avalon cocked an eyebrow. "Wait. You have sisters? How come you've never mentioned them?"

"I haven't seen them in a long time."

"Tell me about it. My brother's a freighter pilot in the Veil, haven't spoken to him in years."

Dash turned to Astrea. "You ready for our big day?"

"Big day?"

"We're going to explore one of the dig sites."

"Like a field trip?"

"Exactly."

"Will I get to see the ruins?"

Dash glanced at Avalon, "I think we can arrange that."

"Sounds like you guys are going on an adventure." Avalon kissed the child on the head, then turned to Dash. "Thanks again for doing this on such short notice."

"You kidding, it's my pleasure."

"You're my hero," Avalon said as the doors shut behind her. Dash glanced at Astrea and a new worry filled her mind. How exactly was she going to investigate an abandoned dig site for anomalous code all day if she had to simultaneously babysit an eight-year-old little girl?

Perhaps she should just wait until tomorrow?

She looked at the trashton in the cleanser, recalling the incident yesterday. No. She'd already waited too long. If her suspicions were correct, every moment counted.

An hour later, Dash and Astrea disembarked the hoverbus at Dig Site Six. Mud squished between her boots as she plodded through the rain toward the entrance. To Dash's dismay, Mother hovered at the turnstile. Dash shook her head. Behind the ton, she spotted the perimeter gate. It surrounded the facility, creating a blockade between the Crimson Forest and the dig site. The red woods reminded her of the cinematic intro from the game last night. The trees resembled a pathway to a forbidden area. Even through her virtual vizard she could smell the distinct stench of the methane ferns. In the distance, thick clouds loomed over the treetops crackling with malice. She'd have to be quick, or else she'd get stuck in this storm.

"Salutations." The hoverton said as the girl approached.

"Salutations?" Astrea turned to Dash, "What's that mean?"

"Response: Salutations is a formal method of saying hello."

Ignoring the ton, Dash scanned the area. Chief Griff was right. The place looked like a ghost town. A graveyard of dilapidated trailers and caravans filled the camp. Abandoned cranes and other heavy equipment lay slumped over like the carcasses of dead animals.

"Wow, look at that!" Astrea stood in awe of the temple before them.

Although Dash knew little about the Daynan culture, she could tell they definitely built things to last. Although the surface had been worn by centuries of weather, the structure still stood tall. "That's where we're going," Dash said, walking toward the monolithic building.

As they approached the temple, Astrea pointed at the opening. "That's as big as an astroship."

"Almost," Dash said. Astrea was right. The opening was enormous. What required such a large entryway in the first place?

"This is so cool," Astrea said, weaving her hover-ball through the scaffoldings that supported the ancient archway. As she passed through the doorway, Dash admired the pillars. Daynan hieroglyphs wrapped around the monolithic stones like vines on a tree trunk. The fact that the architects of these incredible monuments had died so long ago without a trace was a sobering thought. If even the great empires of the past could not withstand the passage of time, what did that mean for modern civilization?

Astrea tugged at Dash's sleeve breaking her chain of thought. "What's wrong with Mother?"

Dash turned to find the admin-drone hovering reluctantly at the entrance.

"Mother, have you ever been in a temple before?"

"Statement: Negative. Our current task will constitute this machine's first experience."

"Don't worry. It's perfectly safe," Dash said walking through the entrance. Mother cautiously followed. The inner temple was more impressive than Dash had anticipated. Several lumistands lit the corridors, revealing countless murals along the walls.

"Wow," Astrea said, staring at the ceiling. "Who are those people?"

"Response: According to myth, the Daynan were the first civilization to traverse the galaxy. Some even believed they were gods that transcended the universe."

"Everyone out here complains about living in Frontier Space, but people back in the Center Sector wish they could see something like this up close." Dash waved her holocom over the control room door. Beep. The doors slid open. "Listen star cake, I have to take care of some work. I don't mind if you look around and play, as long as you stay near the entrance. Deal?"

"Deal," the girl guided her hoverball back toward the pillars.

Dash pursed her lips. She didn't have time to follow the girl around. But it would be a few hours before she finished and she couldn't just expect Astrea to stick with her the whole time. Besides, the automaton had a sensor that could keep tabs on the girl. What's the worst that could happen?

Dash approached the nearest control panel and opened it up for examination. "I suppose we should get to work." She lifted her mask and manually searched for any signs of the mysterious green glyph from yesterday. Nothing. She lowered her visor and plugged in, then reviewed the active scripts running on the machine. Every operating system was like its own little world with unique physics that dictated the interactions of each and every bit and byte. Some were like jungles, where higher-level code fed off of lower-level code. Others were like the ocean, constantly changing with the ebb and flow of information. Programs lived within each of these unique ecosystems. Every program came with its own personality and quirks. Likes and dislikes. Strengths and weaknesses.

Dash swiped her hand along the holo-display, navigating past the surface layer of code. The Cube's system, in particular, behaved like an ant colony. Small programs crawled along pre-designated paths. Soldiers defended the network, workers collected data, scouts searched for information, and one mother-code provided instructions that unified all efforts. Together, they performed as a superorganism, allowing many of the Cube's facilities to run without any human interaction at all. While this structure allowed for optimal efficiency and productivity, it had some flaws. In this system, everything depended on compliance. Every line of code must obey the rules and regulations set forth by governing bodies. But, if code at any level became corrupted, it could cause a major disruption. If one piece of information fell out of line, it could cause a domino effect, trickling through streams of data and infecting others along the way. Each subordinate line would follow suit because it could not think for itself. For this reason, the system was developed with several layers, guidelines, and protocols; safeguards to prevent lower-level organisms from ever communicating with the higher ones. Comparatively speaking, the Cube's code was the most restrictive she'd ever seen, but it was also the cleanest. This made it easy to identify anomalies in the structure.

This particular node displayed nothing out of the norm. Still, probably best to have the ton scan it too. She turned to the admin-drone, "Go ahead and run a diagnostic on this one. Make sure everything's in order."

Mother complied with the request.

As the hoverton scanned the device, Dash looked about the room. A mural on the ceiling caught her eye.

The picture depicted an ominous scene. A great being—a god perhaps? Dash wasn't sure—stood in front of what appeared to be a portal, surrounded by cherubic angels. The deity held something in its hand. Was it a bracelet? Or maybe a necklace? The etching wasn't clear. But energy seemed to be emanating from the jewel within it. In the foreground, several smaller people bowed in reverence. Dash stepped back when she noticed one of the smaller details in the painting. It took her a second to understand what she was looking at. The ground beneath the people in the painting... Were those skeletons? The entire landscape consisted of skulls. Above the ritual, a disc hovered in the sky. Inside the oval, faces of several strange-looking beings peered out, apparently watching the ceremony take place.

"Statement: Diagnostic check complete. The control panel is functioning optimally."

Dash pointed at the mural. "Does the salvage databank have any records on this?"

"Elaboration: Researchers estimate that this is a depiction of realm travel."

An etching written in Daynanic decorated the area below the painting. "What does the glyph say below it?"

Mother scanned the lines. "Interpretation: The symbols represent a warning. According to Daynanic belief, relamic travel held risks. Those who braved the portals did not always return. And if they did, they were not the same."

"Well, that's ominous." She stared back at the control panel. "This one checks out. Let's go hit the others." Hopefully she'd finish soon enough to beat the storm. She wanted to plug-in on time tonight so Dell wouldn't complain. If they got started early enough, they might actually defeat the level and she had a pretty good feeling that this next boss dropped good loot.

Three hours later, Dash finished scanning the final control panel and found no trace of the mysterious code or any anomalous activity. Of course. What a waste of time. She should have just stayed back at the trailer and analyzed the trashton. *Back in my dry, mud-free, air-conditioned trailer,* Dash thought. *Instead, she was out here sweating her aft off in this mucking forest. Lucky me.* As she closed down the holo-interface, Dash tapped the cyber-stylus against her chin. "It just doesn't make sense. Everything points to this dig site. But the system's clean."

Mother hovered closer. "Suggestion: Perhaps the waste management automaton will have more information."

Dash sighed. The admin-drone was right. She glanced at the time. It would be another 15 minutes until the next hoverbus came. "I suppose. But my gut tells me whatever caused the disturbance is here."

Lightning flashed.

Clack-boom.

She peered outside and frowned. The incoming storm blotted out the sky. *Looks like the forecast was right. Time to shut down and call it a day.* She turned to Mother. "Send a message back to headquarters and let them know we're on our way back."

"Statement: This unit is unable to send messages."

"Why not?"

"Response: It appears interference is preventing signals from getting through."

"Well then, let's find Astrea. We'll send the message later." Once they got farther away from the storm, they could attempt to transmit again. She gathered her belongings and started for the exit. The child was nowhere in sight. Maybe she was outside playing in the rain. Dash scanned through the monolithic pillars. Droplets of rain splashed against her virtual vizard as she searched for the child.

"Astrea," she called out.

No response.

She trudged around, calling for the child again.

Still no response.

Where is that girl?

"Mother, where's Astrea?"

"Response: Location unknown. Sensors are unable to detect the child."

Something caught Dash's eye. A glowing round object lay on the ground, just outside of the perimeter fence.

"What's that over there?"

The machine rotated its camcorder-like head and focused its lens in the direction of the glowing object. "Response: Optical receptor identifies it to be a spherical device of some sort."

Dash gripped her cyber-stylus.

"What kind of device?"

The machine clicked. "Clarification: The object is registered as a toy."

She hastened toward the gate.

It wasn't much of a fence. Just grain-link adorned with ultrasonic sirens. Nothing formidable like brick or cinder blocks. But it prevented most creatures from coming through.

As Dash approached, she got a better look at the object. A glowing ball lay on the ground. It pulsed a golden hue against the forest floor. She knelt down to examine it.

"Query: What is it?"

"Hover-ball." Dash picked it up. A butterfly design decorated the device. It definitely belonged to Astrea. What would have possessed that little girl to go beyond the perimeter, and why had she left her hoverball here?

Dash stood up and scanned the area.

"Astrea."

Nothing.

Jam it.

Why did Dash always find herself in these predicaments? She paced the area, then placed her hands on the back of her virtual vizard and took in a deep breath. "This can't be happening."

"Query: Is there a problem?"

Dash gestured to the hover-ball. "That. That is a problem."

Mother cocked its optical receptor to the side. "Confusion: Mother does not understand."

"Astrea. That's her hoverball." She picked up the toy. Tiny footprints led into the trees. "She went into the forest."

The ton fell silent for a moment, apparently processing Dash's comment. "Agreement: Those are logical deductions. Probability is seventy-eight percent that your theory is correct."

Pat. Pat. Pat.

Droplets of rain pitter-pattered against the leaves ahead.

Dash tucked the toy into her cargo pocket as she scanned the treeline. The spike-shaped treetops of the crimson forest pierced the dying rays of the perishing sun. Thorns hung from the bottom branches like the jaws of a bloodthirsty pantra. Below, the bioluminescent brush resembled the twisted innards of a maimed animal carcass. Dash shuttered. What would possess a little kid to go near a place like that?

Then a terrible thought crossed her mind. What if her worst suspicions were true? What if cybots were involved with this code? If so, had she just put Astrea's life in jeopardy by taking her to the dig site? She shook her head. "This *cannot* be happening." Dash activated her utility cuff and scanned for heat signatures in the area. The device bleeped in error.

"Mother, can you detect the girl anywhere?"

The admin-drone hovered in a figure-eight pattern, slowly scanning the surroundings.

"Negative. Sensors are experiencing heavy interference."

Dash closed her eyes. "And you still can't send messages?"

"Affirmative. No signal."

Dash activated her holocom and dialed the emergency line. *Ring.* The line rang. She chewed on her lip as she waited for it to connect. *Bing bong. Shushushush.* The phone beeped then dropped signal. No service. Jam it. She inhaled deeply. "Space scrap. My instruments are all mucked up too." She removed her virtual vizard and looked around. "We'll just have to do this the old fashion way." Child-sized boot prints indented the forest floor. They led along the edge of the tree line. Maybe the kid was nearby, hiding near the bushes? She cupped her hands around the edges of her mouth and shouted, "Astrea? Astrea, are you out there?" No response came. Dash followed the tracks along the treeline and continued to call out.

This is exactly how she wanted to spend her evening: fumbling around the edges of a dark forest in a rainstorm. She examined the ground. A concrete-like brick jutted from the dirt. Dash raked her hands over the debris, pulling away vines and roots. A half-buried statue revealed itself. Dash flinched at the visage staring back at her. Snarled fangs, demonic horns, and bat-shaped wings gave the ruin a gargoyle-like appearance. Behind the structure, a cobblestone road led deeper into the forest.

"Looks like a path."

"Speculation: Perhaps, the child went this way," Mother suggested.

Dash stood up and brushed off her legs. "That's what I'm afraid of. Looks like we'll have to go in after her."

"Warning." Mother spun around and beeped. "The Crimson Forest is off-limits to all personnel."

"I know that. But Astrea could be in danger."

"Suggestion: Company protocols recommend filing a report and waiting for security personnel to assist. Entering the forest is in direct violation of three installation policies."

The machine had a point.

She had heard enough horror stories about the forest to know she didn't want to go in there. At the time, they seemed absurd. Who would be spacey enough to go into a pantra-infested forest? And yet, here she was standing at the edge of the treeline, about to do just that.

She could just imagine how that would affect her transfer request. No doubt that wormhole Buzznard would twist this against her. But if she got lost out here, he would be the last of her worries. On the flip side, Astrea's life was at stake. The girl was likely lost somewhere in these woods. If that was the case, it was imperative to find her as soon as possible. A little kid wouldn't last two seconds in the forest past sundown. Under normal circumstances, Dash would just call this in and wait for security. But, these weren't normal circumstances. Comms were down. The storm was imminent. It could take hours to transmit a message depending on how far the outage reached. Never mind the time it would take for a rescue party to get out here. While Dash hated to admit it, she was Astrea's best chance.

"Response teams will take too long." Dash placed her virtual vizard back on. "We have to go in after her."

Chapter 10: Beyond The Perimeter

"Statement: Dash has been on this path for quite some time, the probability of getting lost is ninety-two percent."

Dash didn't respond. But the ton was right. The last thing she wanted to do was go missing herself. Maybe she *should* turn back.

Crackle. Crackle.

Something rustled in the brush just ahead of them.

Dash froze. The heads-up display on her mask didn't indicate anything out of the norm. "Astrea," she whispered, creeping toward the noise, "Is that you?"

No response. Better get back on the path.

As she headed back toward the path, something caught her eye. A white enviro-helmet lay on the ground, tucked under a thicket. Dash rushed toward it and pulled it out. Astrea's name etched the back of the helmet. "She's definitely out here." Dash examined the helmet. Scratches scarred the surface of the mask. She furrowed her brow. What kind of creature could have made those markings? She had to get a response team out here now. Dash activated her holocom but static filled the other end. Comms were still down. She'd have to physically go back if she wanted to notify the others. If Dash went back now, she could still find the pathway back. Then she could take the hoverbus to digsite five and recruit others to search for the girl. But what would happen if she left Astrea out here all alone? She didn't dare think of what would happen if they didn't find Astrea in time. On the other hand, she could have Mother alert the others while she tried to go after the child on her own. But that was risky too. The last thing she wanted was to get lost out in the woods herself. She had no idea what made those scratches on the girl's helmet and she did *not* want to find out.

Dash had to make a choice and she had to make it fast.

Either go back and tell the others or go deeper into the forest after the girl.

Risky either way.

Scary too.

A memory from her own childhood flashed through her mind. She winced.

No.

No little kid would suffer the way she had—even if it meant Dash had to put herself at risk. She looked to the stars. "Why is it always me? Isn't there anyone else on this mucking planet that can help?"

Dash turned to Mother. "Go back and tell the others we're in the Crimson Forest. Show them the path."

The hoverton tilted its head to one side.

"Query: What about Dash?"

"I'm going to keep looking."

Lightning flashed in the background.

"Estimation: Probability indicates a five percent chance of surviving the night."

"Exactly." Dash gestured toward the forest, "I can't leave Astrea alone out there." She nodded in the direction of the camp. "Now go get me some help."

"Acknowledged." The hoverton swiveled around and fluttered away. Part of Dash actually wanted Mother to stay. While the admin-drone had a knack for annoying her, it also came in handy from time to time. But she knew splitting up was the best chance they had.

Dash activated her mask light and peered into the woods. A chill went down her spine. Roots contorted around the cobblestone walkway and vines twisted down the path. Some snaked into the shrubs, while others slithered up the trees, constricting tree trunks, using fang-shaped thorns to bite into the bark. Above her, branches hung like skeletal remains.

Arrr, arrr, arrrwooo!

A creature howled in the distance.

Why couldn't this have been a computer issue? Codes and viruses that she could do. But the wilderness?

Dash continued forward as darkness swallowed the remaining sunlight. The bioluminescent glow from surrounding bushes illuminated the path. As she trekked further down the walkway, the brush thickened. Even with the help of her heads-up display, it was difficult to navigate the terrain. The path twisted and turned. She tapped on the nav-display. An error message came up:

UNABLE TO CONNECT.

Of course.

She regarded Astrea's mask. Hopefully, she'd be able to find the girl and give it back to her soon. And hopefully Avalon wouldn't freak out when they got back. How would she ever explain this to her best friend? That was assuming they'd ever make it out of here alive. "Maybe Buzz was right. This isn't part of my job description."

Chapter 11: The Crimson Forest

If there was one thing Dash purposely avoided in her daily life, it was physical activity. Not that she was out of shape or anything. To the contrary, she maintained a healthy body weight for her height. She just wasn't a fan of muscle soreness. Or sweaty armpits. Or smelly clothes. But if there was one particular exercise she avoided the most, it was running. Not that she couldn't run. To the contrary. When she served in the Astro Force, she usually scored above average on her PT tests. However, no one ever accused Dash of being an athlete. But back then she never had to run in pitch black of night, or in the mud, or in a thunderstorm. And if there was anything she hated more than running, it was sprinting—especially in mucking woods. Unfortunately, that was exactly her current predicament. Nevertheless, Dash could have overlooked all of those negative aspects, if she wasn't *also* being chased by a wild animal at the same time.

She ducked to a nearby bush and crouched down.

A rustling came from the woods.

What in the realms was that?

She remained perfectly still.

Crackle.

Crackle.

Twigs snapped in the underbrush. *Maybe it's Astrea?* Dash considered calling out, but she heard heavy breathing through the rainfall.

No.

Not breathing.

Panting.

Definitely not Astrea. Some sort of animal lurked nearby.

What was it? A wolfcat? A crockagator? A pantra?

Sunspit.

Have to do something fast.

Two options.

Run.

Or fight.

She wasn't exactly a fighter. But could she really outrun a wild animal?

The panting got closer and the hairs on her neck raised.

She had to move now.

Sprint it is.

Dash lunged forward, moving her feet as fast as she could. And she was quickly reminded why she did not play sports. As with other feats of physicality, running required a certain amount of athleticism. In particular, it required a level of coordination that Dash found herself desperately lacking. Something swiped at her heels and she fell into a pile of leaves.

In that instant, she realized three unfortunate truths. First, running had been a poor decision. Second, the creature definitely knew where she was. Third, it had very sharp claws.

Chapter 12: Alone In The Dark

Dash heard the creature before she saw it.

Arrr, arrr, arrrwooo!

A blood-curdling howl filled the night air. Adrenaline surged through her body as she low-crawled through the shrubbery. Thorns, rocks, and twigs poked and prodded between the soft spots of her enviro-suit. Pain shot down her legs. She ignored it the best she could. Each movement rustled the brush underneath her. But she didn't care. There was no point in being discreet anymore. Despite her discomfort, Dash attempted to stand up.

Something heavy pounced on top of her, slamming her against the ground.

Claws dug into her back.

She'd lost the element of surprise.

Only one option left.

Dash had to stand her ground and fight the beast.

Chapter 13: Oh Drat

Dash was rarely ashamed at her lack of physicality. She knew that her strengths were more intellectual in nature. But when she flung the child's helmet as hard as she could at the creature—and missed completely, she couldn't help but feel a little disappointed.

Nevertheless, she wouldn't give up so easily. Dash swung the helmet again wildly.

The shadowy figure dodged, then leapt in the air. She covered her face and closed her eyes tight. The beast pounced on top of her. Its weight crushed her chest.

Dash never imagined this would be how she died.

In the woods.

Alone.

Searching for a child she was supposed to be babysitting.

She held her breath, anticipating another strike but it never came. Instead, she felt the creature nudge at her elbows.

Dash peaked between her forearms and caught a glimpse of the beast.

What?

She couldn't believe it. The creature wasn't at all what she had imagined.

Not a wolfcat.

Not a spider-bat.

Not a pantra.

It was a... Well, she wasn't quite sure what it was. The closest animal she could liken it to was a drat. Well, mostly anyways. But there was no such thing as drats in real life. They were fictional. Yet, the creature before her was a dog sized lizard with wings.

A wave of relief washed over her as the creature nuzzled into her arms. Dash relaxed her head on the ground, still trying to catch her breath. *Scared of a mucking drat.* Wait till she told the guys about this. Trekking through an actual forest was nothing like the game made it out to be. She'd probably leave out the part about running for her life. What would they think if they knew their archmage was afraid of a little drat? The pet-sized dragon licked her virtual vizard, leaving a streak of slobber along the mask. Apparently the little guy was quite affectionate. *How absurd*, Dash thought. A mucking drat. She chuckled and pain shot through her body. She held her ribcage. *Ouch. Definitely bruised something.* Dash pushed the animal off of her body, then struggled to her feet. As she wiped off her enviro-suit, she looked down at the creature. Its scales sparkled like diamonds under the bioluminescent light, as it ruffled its wings and tucked them back into place.

"You gave me quite a scare there, little guy."

The drat sat on its hind legs and tilted its neck. Its tongue bobbed up and down as it panted.

Dash shook her head.

Some hero you turned out to be.

She placed the helmet in front of the drat. "You haven't seen a little girl around here, have you?"

Wide-eyed, tongue flopping, the animal just stared back at her.

She shrugged. "Worth a shot." Dash examined her surroundings. Nothing seemed familiar and she couldn't find the cobblestone path. Well that was just stellar. *Better keep looking.* She chose a direction at random and started trudging forward. If she continued in a direct line, perhaps she would meet up with Astrea, or the path, or some familiar landmark.

The creature followed. But after a few minutes, it nipped at her heels.

Dash stopped.

The miniature dragon whined.

Maybe it wants food?

She raised her hands, palms up. "Sorry little guy, I don't have anything on me."

Even if she did have a snack, she wouldn't have shared it with the drat. Dash was so hungry, she could eat a whole roast by herself. As soon as she got back to camp, she would eat, bathe, and drink. But maybe in reverse order. After a few more paces, the creature jumped in front of her. Dash stopped and placed her hands on her hips. "*Excuse me.*"

The creature whined and nudged her leg again.

"No food. Sorry," she said, pressing on.

The drat barked at her, then tugged at her boot. Dash tried to shake it off but the animal wouldn't let go. "Sun spit." Dash pulled back with all of her might. The drat released, slingshotting her backward. She fell on her butt and dropped the mask. The drat clawed at it, then shook the helmet back and forth like a rag doll.

"Hey, give that back."

The creature snatched it up, then darted off into the brush.

Dash reached out. "Hey, wait." She rose to her feet and chased after the drat.

"Give that back!"

She followed it up a hill. The dragon traversed the landscape with ease. But each stride felt like someone was adding invisible bricks to her backsack. When they reached the peak, the animal finally stopped. Her lungs burned and her muscles screamed. Maybe this baby dragon would be the death of her after all. Dash rested her hands on her knees, sucking wind. Once she caught her breath, she tapped her nav-display and scanned the area. Still no connection.

Yup.

Lost.

Just what she was trying to avoid.

Not to mention, the drat was nowhere in sight. It must have scurried into the bushes. Now, what the realms would she do? How could she find Astrea? She'd have to backtrack and hope that she could find the cobblestone path. If she ever saw that little mongrel again, she'd turn it into drat soup and then—

"Miss Dash, there you are!" A small voice said.

Chapter 14: Dreams In Ruin

Dash's eyes widened.

Was that a little girl's voice?

Astrea?

Bioluminescent lights glimmered from the treetops, highlighting the child's curly brunette locks. They spiraled down to the top of her shoulders. The girl wore a white enviro-suit that shimmered under the glowing fauna. A pair of blazing blue eyes stared back at Dash. The girl reminded her of one of the cherubic angels from the Daynanic murals they saw earlier. *How in the realms...* It didn't matter. Now that she had found the child, all Dash needed to do was get her back. The drat tramped over to Astrea and dropped the helmet at her feet. The child giggled and stroked the creature's brow.

Dash raised her vizard. "Astrea, thank the stars you're okay," she kneeled down to examine the girl.

The child ignored the comment, choosing to rub the lizard's belly instead. Dash removed the hover-ball and held it in front of Astrea. "I believe this belongs to you."

The child took the toy. "Thanks." She waved it in front of the drat. The creature's eyes followed the ball intently.

She threw it.

"Go get it."

The drat ran off after the toy.

The girl giggled.

"You have no idea how worried I was. Hopefully your mother isn't freaking out right now."

The animal raced back to Astrea with the hoverball in its mouth. She looked down at the drat. "He's a dragon."

Dash smiled. "Oh?" she glanced at the animal, "We've met."

Astrea's eyes went wide and she tugged at Dash's arm. "Miss Dash, I have to show you something!"

Dash didn't budge.

"Honey, we have to get back to camp. Chief Griff probably has every security officer in the colony out searching for us."

The girl hopped up and down and tugged on Dash's arm again. "But I found the best place to play. There's even a lake."

Dash frowned. This kid had no fear at all. She surveyed their surroundings. They couldn't stay too long. But maybe if she placated Astrea for a minute, the girl would come with her. Besides, it's not like they could get any more lost than they already were. "Okay, but once you show me, we need to head back to camp."

The girl nodded, then led Dash through the clearing.

She trudged behind the girl, pushing past brush and tree limbs until they reached a clearing. Astrea ran ahead into the open field. Dash stood dead in her tracks when she saw what lay at the foot of the hill. *Incredible.* She'd never seen such an amazing sight. The treeline formed a perfect circle around a lake. Four ancient pillars surrounded the area. According to her heads-up-display, they were located at each cardinal point, like the notches of a compass. Dash raised her mask. The tranquil water glistened under the red hues of the forest foliage. At the bank closest to them, a horseshoe-shaped archway stood. A platform of some sort sat in the center of the lake. An obelisk shot out from the middle of the structure, like a sword pointing to the heavens. Beyond it, at the far edge of the water, towered the largest tree Dash had ever seen. The bark was white and the leaves gleamed a golden yellow.

"By the stars..."

Astrea skipped toward the archway. Ornate Daynanic designs decorated the monolith. Both sides of the arch converged to a single stone with a circular symbol etched into the face. Vines covered the ancient boulders and intertwined at the base of each side, continuing into the ground like roots, almost as if they had been grafted into the structure purposely.

"Watch this," Astrea said, twisting one of the nearby runes.

Dash raised her hand in protest, "Wait—"

Click. Clack. Clank.

Gears rotated and the lake surface bubbled.

Dash stood perfectly still. What had the child just done?

Sections of ruins emerged from the water and locked into place, connecting all the way from the archway to the platform at the center of the lake, forming a bridge to the obelisk.

Impossible.

Was this a company device?

No. It couldn't be. It was built into the ruins and the symbols on the stones were clearly Daynanic. "That's not possible." The drat snatched the ball from the girl's hand and sprinted down the bridge.

"Come on," Astrea said, following the creature.

"Wait," Dash called out, reaching for the girl. Astrea ignored her and followed the drat down the bridge.Dash hastened after them. They stopped at the end of the platform. As she trotted toward them she noticed symbols along the railing. She pulled out the cyber stylus and scanned a nearby marking. The device blipped, offering a holo-translation and confirming her suspicions. *Definitely Daynanic symbols.* Could this be the source of the anomalous code? Maybe it was a functional ruin? But that's not possible. No one had come across working Daynan tech since the gateways were discovered nearly a century ago.

Astrea stood in front of the obelisk while the drat ran in circles around her. Like the archway, vines wrapped around the monolith. A stone protruded from the base of the structure. It's bowl-like shape reminded Dash of a birdbath.

"Watch this," Astrea said with a mischievous look.

The child wrestled the holo-ball from the drat, then opened it. She dunked it into the lake, then poured the water into the birdbath.

Nothing happened.

"Watch what?"

The child pointed to the bowl. Etchings along the rim started to glow.

Dash stepped back.

"Isn't it super sonic?"

"Yes. Stellar." Dash didn't like the idea of messing around with ancient ruins. She didn't know the first thing about archeology. It was *way* outside of her job description. Then again, if they just stumbled on active Daynan tech, then the company would let her transfer anywhere she wanted. But how did it work?

"How did you know to do that?"

The girl pointed at a glyph just above the ruin. It looked like a cup pouring liquid into the birdbath.

"Oh." Dash examined the stone. Three concentric rings encircled the rim of the bridbath. Chaotic markings decorated each circle and a handle protruded from the outer wheel. She waved the cyber-stylus over the device. Better get as much information as possible. Dash had a feeling the science team would want to see this.

"What is it?"

"Hard to say. No one's come across active Daynan tech in quite some time. The last time was the slideways."

The girl's eyes went wide. "So maybe it's a portal?"

"Don't know." Dash held up the cyber-stylus. "But the sooner we get back, the sooner the archeologists can analyze this data and figure that out."

The girl's brow furrowed. "What's an archeomnogist?"

Dash smiled. "A scientist." She gestured toward the exit. "Now come on. Let's go."

The girl looked down at the ruin. "Awe, do we have to?"

"Yes, we have to."

"But why don't the other marks glow?"

Dash sighed.

The kid was relentless. How did Avalon deal with this on a daily basis? "Astrea, starcake, we need to leave."

Clink. Clink. Clink.

The girl rotated the wheel.

"Hey don't-"

Astrea stopped when the middle-ring markings lined up with the glowing lines from the inner circle.

Click.

The ruin snapped into position. The etchings in the second rung started to glow in concert with those from the first.

"Look. It's like a puzzle."

Dash examined the ruin. "I think you might be right." She folded her arms and tapped the cyber-stylus against her chin. Separately, the markings were scrambled. But together, they might form a symbol. *But of what?*

The girl rotated the wheel again.

Clink. Clink. Clink.

Astrea stopped when several of the outer ring markings lined up with the other two.

Clack.

The ruins rewinded back to the previous position. Astrea glanced at Dash.

Dash nodded. "Try again."

Clink. Clink. Clink.

Clack.

Nothing happened.

Astrea puzzled at Dash. "Miss Dash, why won't it—"

The drat tugged at the holo-ball in Astrea's free hand, wrestling it away and darting down the bridge.

Astrea shook her head. "Why won't it work?"

"I don't know, starcake." She shrugged. "Maybe it needs to line up in a specific order to work."

At the other end of the bridge, the drat barked.

"Will you try?"

Dash glared at the ruin dubiously.

"I don't know. We really should be on our way. Your mother must be worried sick."

The drat barked again.

Astrea ignored the animal and placed her hands together. "Please. Just try one time."

Dash held up her index finger. "Just once."

The child smiled. "Okay. Deal."

Dash glared at the ruin. "Can't hurt to try one time." She pursed her lips. "Right?" She examined the markings. There seemed to be several possible combinations. Who knew which one was right? There was no way Dash could figure it out in one try. But, it didn't really matter. All she had to do was placate the kid, so they could leave.

Behind her, the drat continued to whine. Dash glanced at the mongrel. It sat under the archway and just stared at them. As soon as Dash locked eyes with the drat, it stopped making noises. She shook her head. "This is why I don't have pets." She turned her attention back to the device.

Let's get this over with.

Dash gripped the handle ready to turn it, but something caught her eye.

She cocked her head. "Wait."

Through the water, she could see a symbol on the face of the bowl. Dash leaned in. It looked familiar. Like glyph, she'd seen recently. Maybe on one of the other ruins?

"What is it?" Astrea asked.

"I think we've seen this somewhere before."

Dash scanned the glyphs that ran up the obelisk.

No. Not there.

Her eyes followed the railing along the bridge.

Nothing there either.

"What about those big rocks?"

Dash raised a finger. "No. Just give me a second."

She surveyed the area. It was around here somewhere. She was sure of it.

The drat barked again.

Dash's shoulders clenched. How could she concentrate with all of this racket? Why did the animal insist on barking at them? Shouldn't it be out hunting vermin or something? It barked again. Dash clenched her jaw and glared at the drat. It stopped barking again. "I swear by the stars I'm going to put that beast out of its..."

Wait.

Something caught her eye.

What's that?

Dash squinted.

Yes.

There it was, just above the Drat. The same symbol etched in the archway resembled the one at the bottom of the birdbath. Had the animal been trying to point that out the whole time? *Impossible. No reptile is that intelligent.* Dash pointed her cyber-stylus at the glyph. "I think it's the same symbol as that one."

She looked back at the wheel. If she just rotated it a few times counterclockwise, the markings might line up and recreate the full symbol. But was that something she really wanted to do? Dash paused. Tampering with active Daynan tech probably violated a few company regulations. If Mother were here, Dash was sure the admin drone would be listing each one of them off in that annoying monotone voice it had. And who knew what the ruin would do if she actually activated something. Not to mention, they really needed to get back to the dig site. This place was not safe. Dash chewed at her lip. On the other hand, if she was right, this could be a huge discovery. The primes would want to know as much about it as possible. The more information she had, the more valuable an asset she would be to the company. This could finally be her chance to free herself from Buzz and this wretched planet.

Yes.

That would be stellar.

Maybe it was worth the risk?

Dash gripped the handle and took a deep breath. "Here we go."

She turned the wheel counterclockwise. She had to rotate it several times before it organized into the right configuration. Each of the markings seemed to connect with a corresponding line on the adjacent rings. Dash glanced at the archway glyph. The symbols seemed to match. "Here goes nothing."

She let go.

Click.

The ruin snapped into position and all of the markings started to glow, including those at the bottom of the bowl.

Astrea threw her hands up. "You did it!"

The rungs lowered and the water drained into the vines of the ruin like blood flowing through a vein. Then all of the symbols on the obelisk lit up. *Whirrr.* The structure hummed in response and a spherical form emerged from the birdbath. Was that water? Dash inched away from the device.

What had she done?

"Look," Astrea said, pointing at the lake.

Dash spun around and could not believe her eyes.

The lake water had morphed into a sphere. It looked just like a holo-image but made out of water.

By the stars.

"What is it?"

"Some sort of water tech. Like a holo-display." Dash tilted her head. "An aqua-display, I would guess."

"Is it a picture?"

Dash squinted. The girl was right. It appeared to be a three-dimensional image. She could see rudimentary shapes and colors. But the details were hard to make out. The display seemed out of focus. Dash shrugged. "Maybe it's Daynan art?"

Astrea walked back to the birdbath shaped ruin and placed her hand into the liquid sphere. The water cascaded over her fingers like a waterfall. "Isn't it cool?"

The lake image fizzled into static.

"Wait. Go back."

Astrea removed her hand and the water reformed into a sphere. The lake image followed suit.

Interesting. Was the birdbath an interface for the lake water? Dash removed her cyber stylus, "A wizard's job is never done." She waved the device as if it were a wand, scanning the aqua-display. "Science team will want to see this too."

The child splashed her hands in the aqua-interface.

The picture zoomed in.

Then out.

Then in, again.

But the image was still unfocused.

Dash clicked her cyber stylus back into the utility cuff.

"Can I try?" she asked, approaching the birdbath shaped stone.

The girl backed away. "Sure. It's super fun."

Dash placed her hands in the water. Nothing happened.

Strange.

Why did it work for the girl?

She examined Astrea's hands, then her own. The girl wasn't wearing the gloves to her enviro-suit. Did the device require skin contact? *Worth a shot.* Dash removed her glove and placed her hand in the water. The cold liquid streamed through her fingers and the image came into perfect focus. Dash's eyes went wide. Lines and lines of the anomalous code filled the lake's aqua-display. "Woah," Astrea said, "how'd you get it to do that?" Dash was no xenolinguist, but they seemed to be looking at a message in the aqua-display. Or maybe it was a list? She couldn't tell. A few sections were highlighted and certain symbols blinked red.

Dash adjusted her hand and the words scrolled. What is this? Did the display react to her movements?

Interesting.

"Now I want to do it." Astrea thrust her hand into the water.

An electric-like current zapped through Dash's fingertips and shot down her spine all the way to her toes. Her teeth stung and her nose burned. Each muscle in her body clenched, paralyzing her. Dash strained with every sliver of strength she could muster to pull their hands out of the water, but the interface would not release them.

Astrea cried out in terror.

From the corner of her eye, Dash saw the child's body go limp.

The aqua-interface exploded, throwing Dash to the ground. Her virtual vizard cracked against the ruins, then her heads-up display fizzled into nothingness. She tried to get up, but her body failed her. She craned her neck toward Astrea. The girl lay motionless on the ground. Was she dead? Dash couldn't tell, but the look on the child's face resembled her sisters when they died. As she fell into the blackness of unconsciousness, a wave of relief splashed over her. Soon she would be dead and perhaps, if she was lucky, she'd be reunited with her sisters at long last.

Then the world spun into oblivion.

Chapter 15: Mission Impossible

Mother fluttered around the hoverbus station anxiously. According to the installation schedule, the last bus of the day should have arrived ten minutes ago. But it had not shown up. *Where are they?* Given today's weather forecast, there was a high probability that stops to dig site six were canceled on account of the storm surge.

The machine attempted to connect with headquarters.

Ring.

Ring.

Blip.

The signal dropped.

Barcodes and bitmaps. Where was the bus?

Mother would have to get closer to dig site five before it could catch a signal. That meant the admin-drone would have to hover on its own at significantly slower speeds than the hoverbus. But if it left and the hoverbus arrived, Mother would miss the opportunity to connect with the vehicle's longer-range transmission instruments. Given current battery levels, wind speeds, and atmospheric conditions, its processor estimated a minimum of 13 minutes before it could get in range to make a call. Would that be soon enough to help Dash? Every minute the server farmer spent in the Crimson Forest decreased the probability of her survival. The automaton wondered whether or not Dash found the little girl and if they were safe. Although the machine did warn Dash against treading into the woods alone, the probability that this unit would be held accountable for any mishaps that might arise was still high.

Mother turned toward Dig Site Five.

Something rustled in the brush next to the benches. The hoverton spun around to face the noise. When the admin-drone's optical receptor identified the origin of the sound, nothing could have prepared the machine for what it saw next.

Chapter 16: Worst Headache In The World

Dash's forehead throbbed and the smell of burnt metal singed her nostrils.

She opened her eyes.

Still alive?

She sat up and rubbed the back of her neck. Her skull felt like it was going to explode. *What in the Twelve Realms just happened?* She surveyed the area. Astrea sat next to her, head in hands, sobbing. Scattered remains of the aqua-interface littered the platform. The obelisk lay beside them, snapped in half like a twig. Dash shuddered to imagine what would have happened if it had fallen toward them rather than away.

"You okay star cake?"

The child blinked away tears. "I'm sorry."

Dash smiled. "That's okay, honey. I'm just glad no one was hurt." The girl stared into the distance, apparently ignoring Dash's comment. She kneeled before the child, "But we really do need to leave."

Astrea nodded, then wiped her cheeks.

"Stellar. Let's get going." Dash helped the girl up and wiped off the child's enviro-suit.

Dash checked her holocom.

Static filled the device.

Sunspit. Still no signal.

They couldn't stay here all night. It was too dangerous. But if they held position, it might make it easier for rescue teams to find them. But who knows how long that would take? And the explosion might have attracted unwanted attention. Not to mention, there was a chance that Mother may not have made it back to the dig site to warn the others. Dash would have to make a decision.

The girl tugged at her arm. "Miss Dash, I'm hungry."

Dash frowned. To be completely honest, Dash was starving too. "Me too. The sooner we get back, the sooner we can eat." The longer they stayed out here, the more likely trouble would find them. And Dash learned long ago not to wait for help. *Wait.* Something caught the corner of her eye. Her virtual vizard. It sat cracked at the corner of the ruins. They walked down the platform and through the archways, then picked up the mask. *How in the Twelve Realms will we find our way back?* She could not begin to imagine how they would make it to the installation. Astrea held Dash's hand. The child's tiny digits felt small and cold against her palm.

She smiled back at the girl.

We'll figure it out.

When she left dig site six, the nav-display said they were heading North. She glared at the dog-sized lizard. But during her encounter with the drat, she'd lost her bearings. Nevertheless, if they headed South long enough, there was a good chance they would come across a familiar landmark.

She nodded in a Southward direction, "Okay. Let's get going."

Chapter 17: At Least Things Can't Get Worse

They trudged through the brush for at least half an hour. Despite her attempts to lose the confounded thing, the drat followed them through the woods. The animal flew overhead, occasionally hopping from treetop to treetop. Dash's body ached and her stomach burned. This was more physical activity than she'd done in quite some time. Sweat dripped through crevices in the enviro-suit. Tonight ranked as one of the top ten worst evenings of her life. But at least things couldn't get any worse. Fantasies of a bath and glass of wine danced in her head as they pressed on. *Just have to get back.* Then she could plug-in and call it a night.

Psshh.

Psshh.

Snap.

Psshh.

Psshh.

The leaves rustled and a branch snapped ahead of them. Dash pulled Astrea close. She couldn't imagine how this day could get any worse.

She was about to find out.

They both froze.

Astrea's tiny hand tightened in hers.

"It's okay," Dash whispered. But she knew that was far from true. Something lurked in the woods just ahead and it didn't sound like a rescue party. Dash placed her arm in front of Astrea and pushed the child behind her. The girl clung to Dash's leg. As they inched backward, she considered their options. They could stand their ground, flee, or hide. Dash didn't think she could put up much of a fight, especially with a child in tow. But she wasn't sure how fast she could run with the girl either. She glanced at the drat. Running didn't exactly work out very well for her the last time she tried.

Hiding was their best bet.

Dash led Astrea into a nearby thicket. Thorns pricked and branches prodded as they ducked into the bushes.

Snap.

Crack.

Pop.

Leaves sifted as a shadow emerged from the woods ahead. Lips curled, fangs bared, wings erect, the drat crouched into an attack position and growled at the specter. Whatever approached, the drat did not like it.

Could it be a member of a rescue team?

Doubtful.

Maybe another drat?

The shadow prowled toward them, bringing the creature's merlot-colored musculature into full view under the bioluminescent rays of the foliage. In that moment, the deepest form of carnal dread she had ever felt gripped her. Astrea gasped aloud and Dash placed a hand over the girl's mouth, ducking deeper into cover. The beast was definitely not another drat, or part of a rescue team. Or, anything friendly for that matter.

Chapter 18: Pantra Pickings

It was hate at first sight.

The drat lept toward the bushes, ready to fight.

Dash couldn't believe her eyes.

Before her, a pantra the size of a hovercar advanced on their position. Their scaley companion circled to the side of the monster, barking, and yipping. The beast stalked toward the lizard and growled. The dragon stood on its hind legs and expanded its wings to full span, then hissed back. The pantra swatted at the drat. It fluttered to the side, then nipped at the creature's heels. The pantra released a deafening roar.

The drat was going to get itself killed. *And us along with it*, Dash thought.

Astrea tried to pull away, but Dash held her close. The girl looked back at her but Dash shook her head. Astrea's lip quivered uncontrollably. There was nothing they could do to help. That monster would eat them alive.

Snraarrrr.

The pantra snarled at the dog-sized reptile, then backed away. Pressing with his attack, the drat continued to bark and push the beast backward.

Strange. Why didn't the pantra attack? Dash squinted. Was it dazed? The animal swayed and wobbled, as if it were drunk, then collapsed to the ground.

The drat tilted its head, then looked back to Dash as if waiting for an explanation. She wanted one too. What the stars just happened?

Astrea darted out of the thicket.

Dash reached for her but couldn't catch her in time.

The girl hugged the drat.

"You saved us! What a good boy!"

The animal licked her face and wagged his tail.

Dash waved the girl in. "Astrea! Get back over here," she said in a hushed voice.

The girl ignored her and continued to pet the drat.

Jam it.

Dash navigated out of the underbrush and walked over to the girl. Something didn't add up. She wasn't an animal expert, but she was pretty sure that a pantra could fight off a whole pack of wolfcats, nevermind this little dog-sized lizard. So, what in the stars just happened? As she inched closer, Dash could see the pantra's ribcage rise and fall with each breath. A wheezing noise followed each exhalation. Was it snoring? No, that made no sense. The animal couldn't have just fallen asleep in the middle of a fight.

Their winged companion circled the pantra, sniffing the beast's body. It appeared to be just as confused as Dash.

Then she saw it.

Oh no.

Dash knew exactly why the animal seemed to be asleep. The situation was far worse than she had imagined. She picked up the child and raced back to the thicket. They had to get to cover right now.

"Miss Dash, it's okay. The dragon took care of that big monster."

"No. He didn't honey."

"But it's laying on the ground right there."

"That's because it was hit with a tranquilizer."

Chapter 19: What's A Trankalaster?

"What's a trankalaster?"

Dash didn't answer. She grabbed Astrea's hand and led her into the forest. The drat darted off in the other direction. Where did he think he was going? It didn't matter. They had to get out of here as soon as possib—

"Bzzzarttnatzzat."

Dash froze.

Lightning flashed against the crimson treetops, illuminating the forest and revealing a group of fly-faced aliens; the Bush People. A chill trickled through Dash's veins. Although she'd never seen a buzzer up close, she had attended enough security briefings to know that she did not want to. The four-armed flesh eaters emerged from the bioluminescent foliage, equipped with primitive armor and technosticks. Raindrops fizzled against the taser-tipped weapons, as they converged on Astrea's position. Without thinking, Dash stepped in front of the girl. How in the realms would they get out of this mess? If Dash didn't come up with something quick, the raiders would turn her and the kid into star soup.

A heads-up display would have come in handy right about now. But that mucking explosion back at the ruins totally smoked her virtual vizard. Now she only wore the mask to keep the rain out of her eyes. And where exactly was the admin-drone? She sent that bucket of bolts back for help hours ago. Apparently, Dash and Astrea were all on their own, which meant she'd have to improvise. Dash raised her hands. "We don't want any trouble."

The lead alien pointed at Astrea and buzzed orders in an indecipherable language. The other three attackers raised their technosticks and gave acknowledgement. Their voices grated against her ears like a garbled microphone. Were they wearing facemasks? Dash couldn't tell.

Astrea inched backward, "Miss Dash, I'm scared."

"See star cake, this is why we can't go following dragons into the woods."

"Yes, ma'am."

The buzzers pressed forward.

Dash picked up a fallen branch and pointed it at the closest assailant. "Back off bug breath." She swung the makeshift weapon wildly. Snap. The front section of the stick went limp, then fell into the mud. The alien cocked its head, looked to the forest floor and back at Dash, then thrust his technostick at her.

Dash bobbed her head out of the way.

The electrified fork came micrometers from her mask.

She threw the remaining piece of wood at him.

It missed, completely.

Of course.

She grabbed Astrea's hand, "Get your aft in gear kid!" she shouted, then pulled the child into the bushes.

As they weaved through the maze of glowing brush, Dash couldn't help but think how entirely astro this whole situation was. She was an automaton manager for star's sake. By all rights she should be sitting at her workstation, sipping coffee and reviewing code. Not getting chased by rag-wrapped aborigines in a dark forest during the middle of a thunderstorm.

Clack. Boom.

A bolt of lightning struck a nearby tree. Dash's foot snagged a root. Or, maybe it was a rock? She couldn't be sure. Either way, found herself falling face first into a thicket of thorns. As she braced for impact, Dash wondered how her boring life had come to this? Just yesterday she had been working on the server farms in the basement of the Hestia facility without a care in the world.

It was all those salvager's fault. She should have left that portal alone. Then she wouldn't be in this mess.

Dash scrambled to her feet and looked for Astrea.

Two buzzer's held the girl by the arms, while a third pointed a technistick at her. The fourth approached Dash, weapon raised.

At that moment Dash realized one thing was for certain. She would never agree to babysit again.

Chapter 20: The Electric Slide

"Bzzzattzzzat."

The leader pointed at her, speaking to his companions in an unintelligible language. They responded in more garbled words. Sounded like flies buzzing, but through a muffled microphone.

This day definitely did not turn out the way she had imagined. Not in the least.

She recalled the tranquilized pantra. If they could take out a beast that size, they could surely make short work of Dash. How in the Twelve Realms could she defend against them?

The closest fly-man lunged at Astrea and attempted to grab her.

Grrrrr.

The drat jumped between them and growled at the assailant.

"Nice of you to show up," Dash said under her breath, retreating further back.

The alien gave a muffled shout and kicked at the dragon. The animal dodged, then nipped at his heels. The bushman swung his techno-stick. The drat evaded the blow, scurried up a tree, then leapt on top of the alien, scratching and clawing at his face. A second alien raced over to help his comrade.

Another buzzer advanced toward Dash. Sunspit. She inched back. If only there were something she could use to fight them off.

"Let me go," Astrea struggled against the other two buzzers. In the background, she watched the drat pounce on top of the first bushman, gnawing at its facemask.

It's comrade swatted the dragon with his techno-stick.

Zap.

The dragon fell to the ground.

"No," Astrea squeaked.

She'd have to steer clear of the techno-sticks.

Or did she?

An idea popped into Dash's mind. She activated her utility cuff and locked on to all three staffs. The lead alien raced toward her, weapon raised, ready to strike. Dash pressed the button. Zrrraaaap. The bug-eyed terror stopped in its tracks, arms jittering and knees wobbling. His techno-stick surged with an electric charge. The current connected to his comrade's staff, emitting arcs that looked like electric rainbows. The energy hopped down the row of assailants, until each of the fly-like aliens contorted and knelt to the ground.

Yes. It worked! Dash couldn't believe it worked.

The leader released his technostick and stood back up, visibly enraged.

No.

The assailant charged at her.

Wham.

The bioluminescent tree-tops flipped upside down. Smack. Dash hit the ground hard. Needles of pain stabbed at her chest. A firm three-fingered grip forced her onto her back. Two bulbous black orbs glared back at her. A stench of feces assailed her nostrils as he tied her hands together with what looked like a forest vine. She gagged. Astrea cried out. Dash railed against the bushman, but could not break free. This can't be happening. Her attacker rummaged in his pouch, digging for something. What's he doing? Familiar needle-shaped objects fell out of the pouch and onto the ground. Tranq darts. He grabbed one of the needles. Was he going to tranquilize her?

Dash pushed against him with all of her might.

Then, a nightmarish shriek filled the forest.

The bushman froze, then turned his head in the direction of the noise, suddenly unconcerned with Dash. She wriggled her arms free and pushed him off, then rolled up to a kneeling position. The attacker stood still, with the tranq dart still raised, as if he was weighing out a decision.

More shrieks filled the air.

One of the aliens shouted. Dash sensed a hint of urgency in his tone.

The brush rustled behind her. Something was coming—several somethings. Her heart sank. Was it another pantra? Or maybe more bush people? Shrieks filled the night air.

The leader buzzed out orders and all four bushmen retreated into the forest without a second glacé at Dash, Astrea, or the drat. What's going on? She rushed to Astrea, who knelt down next to the drat. They still seemed dazed.

"Are you okay?"

Tears streamed down the child's face. She nodded.

Shroooct. Shroooct. Shroooct.

Throat clenching shrieks filled the forest.

Now what?

Dash scanned the woods. She had assumed her night couldn't possibly get worse. Like what were the odds that someone would run into a pantra, then Bush People in the one night anyway? But after she saw the origin of the shrieks, she realized she was wrong. It could get worse.

It was worse.

Way worse.

Chapter 21: What The Flock

Perhaps their chances would have been better with the Bush People. There was only one thing in the world that could possibly be worse than a bloodthirsty pantra or aboriginal bushmen, and Dash was staring right at it. She could not believe her eyes. The treetops seemed to crawl. Hundreds of rat-sized creatures flocked through the branches.

Oh no. *It can't be.* She squinted and confirmed her worst fear. *Spider-bats.* Not one. Not two. But a whole flock of spider-bats. The poisonous arachnids flapped their hairy wings, leaping from branch to branch.

It was worse than any nightmare she'd ever had.

It was no wonder the buzzers ran.

Dash had no idea how they would get out of this. But then, something even more bizarre happened.

The area around the spider bats blurred like an out of focus holo-vid. Then the eight-legged pests wavered in and out of transparency, until they evaporated into a mist.

By the stars.

What just happened?

A stranger emerged from the underbrush where the winged terrors crawled just seconds ago. For a split second, Dash thought it was a female bushman. She reflexively winced at the sight of the woman's multiple eyes and buglike features.

But when the stranger stepped into the light, Dash realized she had been mistaken. The woman was clearly human. Strange. The tree shadows must have distorted the old lady's face. The woman used a walking stick to help her sift through the bushes. Dash squinted. Correction, the woman used a walking stick with one hand and pointed a weapon directly at them with the other.

Dash placed her hands in the air.

The stranger traced the area with her weapon. Wait, was it a gun? Dash couldn't quite tell. She wasn't a weapons expert. But it didn't resemble any type of blazer she'd ever seen. It looked like a mini-crossbow attached to the woman's wrist. With a bend of her elbow, the weapon transformed and holstered itself into her utility cuff. "Well, that was lucky," she said in a matter-of-fact tone.

Dash noticed an exotic accent when the newcomer spoke. Kind of like the one that vampires had in the horror shows she watched as a kid. Dash tilted her head. Who was this shaman?

Dash lowered her hands. "Thanks."

The woman gave a warm smile.

Dash brushed off the leaves and dirt from her envirosuit. "So, who-"

Ruff. Ruff.

The drat barked, then raced over to the newcomer and licked at her hand.

The woman kneeled down and patted the drat. "Arkery, so that's where you have been."

"Arkery?" Astrea asked.

The woman nodded at the girl. "That's his name."

"Is he your pet?"

The woman tilted her head and peered at the treetops. "Sort of. Are you familiar with the term, 'familiar.'"

The girl looked confused. "What's a familiar?"

Buzzing shouts echoed in the forest. The newcomer squinted. "We should not linger. I fooled the Bush People once, but that is unlikely to happen again." She nodded at the pantra, still lying unconscious on the ground. "Not to mention, we will want to leave before this guy wakes up." She picked up a dart from the grass and knelt next to the predator.

Dash raised her hand, "I wouldn't do that if I were you."

With one swift jab, the stranger injected the tranquilizer into the beast's haunches. "That should buy us some time. He's more valuable to them than we are." The shaman collected the rest of the darts and placed them into her utility sack, "We will hold on to these just in case we run into any more unwelcome guests."

Chapter 22: The Spride

Rain drizzled as Dash and her companions trekked in silence. They followed the shaman's lead. She seemed to know where she was going. Arkery swooped from branch to branch in the treetops above, while Astrea stuck to Dash's side. The cut on Dash's chest throbbed from her scrape with the bushman. Fatigue overtook her body and she worried that she might pass out from exhaustion. Only fear and hunger kept her going. She had no idea who the stranger was, or if she could help them find their way back to the installation, but they didn't really have any other options and the woman seemed to know where she was going. Every so often the shaman would retrieve what appeared to be an old-timey paper notebook from her satchel, examine it, then change direction. Was there a map in the notebook? If so, why didn't the woman use a holopad? But that also seemed unlikely. According to all of the security briefs she'd ever attended, most of the forest was still uncharted. To be fair, Dash slept through most of those presentations, so perhaps there was something she'd missed.

The stranger reviewed her notepad again. "How did you get so far into the forest?"

"It's a long story. I had to go check some control panels at dig site six. But my friend needed me to watch her daughter."

Astrea waved. "That's me."

"So, I brought her along. But then she went missing and the storm rolled in about the same time. One thing led to another, and now here we are."

"And?"

"And what? That's it."

"I thought you said it was a long story."

Dash furrowed her brow. "I guess it wasn't that long of a story afterall. Just felt like one."

The woman hiked onward without commenting.

Dash regarded her rescuer. Was she one of the colony scientists? Doubtful. Most colonists didn't dress like that, nevermind carry around firearms or... walking aids. What Dash initially had identified as a hiking stick was actually a slate colored staff. Intricate designs decorated the device from top to bottom. The midsection emitted an energy field of some sort. Not to mention, the stranger's outfit was as exotic as her weapons. It almost looked Varelean. But the woman was clearly human. Her clothing had a tribal feel to it, giving the old lady an almost shaman-like appearance. Her vizard was reminiscent of a priestess' headdress. Several metal pieces shaped like feathers were crafted into an intricate design, making the suit look almost phoenix-like. Braids of hair ending in decorative beads hung like ornaments on either side of her face.

Who exactly was this woman?

"So, you're part of the science team?"

"In a manner of speaking," she wiped off her hand on her animal-skin tasset then offered it to Dash, "I am Lera. Lera Nightingale."

Astrea cut in front of Dash and tugged at the woman's arm, "My name is Astrea."

The woman smirked, "Astrea. That is a beautiful name."

Lera Nightingale. Why did that name sound familiar?

The woman bent down, "Let me take a look at you." She examined the girl. "Not a scratch. You must be quite the fighter."

"Yeah, but Mrs. Dash helped a little."

A little!? The kid had quite the imagination.

"Is that so?" Lera glanced up at Dash. "Dash? Would that be the same employee 1-X, who rescued salvagers at Dig Site four yesterday?"

Dash nodded. "Word travels fast, apparently."

"This is a small installation, and you are the hero of the day."

Yeah right. A hero that got lost in the forest, blew up a ruin, almost got eaten by a pantra, and was nearly murdered by Bush People. Dash was hardly a hero. Also, she decided that she probably shouldn't mention that part about blowing up the ruins.

"So, you were examining control panels at Dig Site Six. Might I ask why?"

"Yesterday's mishap at Four seems to have been caused by a virus. I had reason to believe it originated at Six."

"And did you find anything?"

All of a sudden Dash felt like she was being interrogated. She wasn't sure how much information she should give this stranger. On the flip side, there wasn't really anything of significance to tell. "Nothing."

Lera's brow furrowed. Was the shaman suspicious of something? Probably best to change the subject. "So, how did you find us? This isn't exactly the type of place someone goes out for an evening stroll."

"I ran into your hoverton. It said you needed help. I instructed it to head back and notify security."

"Mother? Looks like that admin-drone turned out to be good for something after all." But that didn't explain how Lera found them. They could have been anywhere in the forest. How did she know to come to that exact location?

The drat scurried down the tree and nuzzled Dash.

Lera nodded, "He likes you."

Dash frowned. "It just kind of followed us."

Astrea held her hands together as if begging. "I want to take him home."

"Absolutely not, young lady. Your mother's already going to kill me."

Lera leaned in toward the girl. "You know, the Daynan believed that scaleens were descendants of dragons."

Astrea's eyes went wide. "Really?"

"According to legend, they traveled back to their home realm of Ektosia."

"Where's that?"

"Outside of time and space," Dash said. "The Extramural realm."

Lera raised a finger, "It sounds like Miss Dash knows her Realmic history. They say that only the most devout know the realms by name."

Dash waved her hand dismissively. "Not religious. Just an avid fantasy reader."

The older woman cocked an eyebrow. "Indeed." The woman glanced at Astrea. "Did you know that books were the first form of realm travel?"

The girl shook her head.

"It's true. Books act as a bridge between worlds and allow people to communicate between time and space. But just like the pyramids, modern man has forgotten their true function."

"We saw a pyramid," Astrea said.

Lera placed her hands on her hips. "Did you now?"

"That was a ruin starcake, not a pyramid," Dash corrected.

"Yeah, a ruin, on the lake. It was so stellar." Astrea raised her hands. "The water was like a holocom and there were these strange *symbols* everywhere." She lowered her head. "But we broke it."

The stranger frowned at the little girl. "Broke it?" She turned to Dash. "You mean the platform by the great tree?"

Dash pursed her lips. As cute as the girl was, she sure had a big mouth. "There was some kind of active Daynan tech there," Dash said. "Like an aqua-interface."

"Indeed," Lera said neutrally. "Several ancient secrets lie hidden in those ruins. Most are best left alone."

"Agreed," Dash said. The mishap was so recent, she could still feel her skin tingling from that surge of power.

"So, you interacted with the ruin?"

Dash shrugged. "I mean we got the image to focus. That's about it." She pulled out her cyber-stylus and handed it to the woman. "I took some scans. Figured the scientists would be able to make sense of it."

Lera gave Dash a scrutinizing look. She couldn't be sure, but it seemed like she was being assessed. After a moment, the woman nodded and took the device. "Indeed." She transferred the data to her own device, then handed it back to Dash.

"Is that a spider?" Astrea asked, pointing to the symbol on Lera's armor. To Dash, it looked like a spider in the middle of a web."

Lera smiled. "It is." The woman lowered her staff. "You see this?" She pointed to an amulet at the top of the device. It looked like a dreamcatcher, with the same symbol of a spider in the center of a web. "This is the same symbol. It's the emblem of my order. The order of the Spride."

"What does it mean, miss Lera?"

"How many legs does a spider have?"

Astrea looked to the sky, searching for an answer. "Um... Eight. Spiders have eight legs."

"Correct. Snappy girl. Each limb represents the high priests of our order. And that web represents the Realmverse."

Astrea tilted her head. "I don't think I understand."

"See how the web is interwoven and each strand connects to another?"

The girl nodded her head.

She pointed at the strands. "The realms are connected to each other, just like this web. If something happens to one, the others are affected."

Dash maneuvered around a tree branch. "Can't say I've ever heard of the Spride before."

The woman raised her staff. "We are the keepers of ancient knowledge, charged with the responsibility of maintaining order within the realms."

"Sounds like a big job. But what does it have to do with the Hestia colony? Are you part of the science team?"

"I am more of a…" Lera rocked her head side to side, "…consultant."

"I want to be in the Spride," Astrea said.

Lera laughed. "Indeed. Well, in order to even be considered, every candidate has to solve a riddle."

"I love riddles. Miss Lera, give me the riddle."

"Okay. Okay." The woman stopped and held her hands out. "Which hand has the power to change the world?"

Astrea puzzled at the woman's hands for a moment, then picked the right one.

Lera shook her head.

"So it's that one?" the girl guessed, pointing to the left hand.

The stranger glanced at Dash. "What do you think?"

Dash wasn't great at riddles, nor was she in the mood for games. Quite frankly, the only power she'd ever seen resided with the conglomerate. "I think I'm tired, and hungry, and sore. And, that we should get back to the dig site as soon as possible."

Lera gave a curt smile. "Indeed. Right you are." She glanced at Astrea, "I am afraid we must make haste child."

Astrea frowned.

They continued to trek in silence for several more minutes. Dash got the impression that Lera was ruminating on their conversation. Hopefully, Dash hadn't said something that would reflect poorly on the company. Given the fact that she took scans of the incident, the science team should still be able to analyze the data.

The forest opened up and they came across the cobblestone path from earlier. She could see the perimeter lights of Digsite

Six in the distance. How did Lera find their way back so quickly? A hoverbike sat in the brush just ahead. Lera hopped on the vehicle. "This path will lead you back." She unfastened her utility pack and tucked it away in the hoverbike's rear compartment. In the distance, sirens blared. "Sounds like a rescue team is on the way."

Better late than never.

Lera leaned in, "Listen, they will want a report about what happened. Do not mention what you saw in the aqua-interface."

"*Okay*? Why?"

Lera glanced about, then leaned in and whispered, "It may not be wise to discuss the details at this point in time."

Dash tilted her head. Details? Was Lera talking about the image from the lake ruins? What was the scientist not telling her? Did this mean that Dash's concerns about the anomalous code were warranted? If so, how did she know she could trust this woman?

Lera must have sensed her hesitation because she said, "We will talk soon. Just, trust me on this."

She did save your life. And, the scientist would know way more about the ruins than you do. Dash nodded. "Okay." She didn't like not knowing. But she understood that situations like this required a certain level of discreteness.

Astrea tugged at Lera's arm. "You're not coming with us?"

"I have a few more things to take care of, little one."

"So was it the other hand?"

"Was what the other hand?"

"The riddle."

"Ah yes, that." The shaman took Astrea's hands into hers. "These are the hands that can change the world."

Astrea smiled.

"Are you going to change back into those flying spiders?"

The scientist smirked, "No, little one, not again. Now, I am sure it is past your bedtime. Go, get some sleep."

"How *did* you do that by the way?" Dash asked. The question had bothered her ever since they escaped the bush people. She figured it had to be a projection code of some sort. Dash herself had spells that would allow her holocom to create a single decoy. But she'd never seen one that could interact with an entire environment at such a large scale. In order to achieve such a feat, one would have had to implant multiple holo-displays within the trees, which couldn't be possible because the location that the Bush People attacked from was completely random. There was no way that the scientist could have predicted exactly where they would be. "How did you project all of those images at once? What code did you use?"

The woman secured her staff to the vehicle. "It is a special program known only to savants," she said dubiously.

Dash tilted her head. "Savants?"

Lera nodded, activated the hoverbike and sped off. Arkery, lept in the air and followed.

"Thanks for the help," Dash mumbled to herself. As she watched them disappear into the distance, a new question filled her mind. What the hack was a savant, and how could she get access to a code like that?

Dash grabbed Astrea's hand and headed for the dig site.

"I can't wait to tell mommy about our adventure. Do you think she'll be mad that we stayed out so late?"

Dash's eyes went wide. She could only hope that Avalon wouldn't be too upset with her. After all, Astrea had run off on her own. *But you were supposed to be watching the girl.* She glanced at Astrea. It couldn't be that big of a deal, right? All Dash did was lose the girl during a thunderstorm, in the middle of a dark forest, filled with wild animals... before nearly blowing the child up at an ancient ruin site. Not to mention they came face-to-face with a pantra, then had a run in with violent fly aliens.

"Yeah, no. I'm sure Avalon won't be upset at all."

It's funny how a near death experience helps you overlook all of the stupid scrap that used to bother you. As medtons scanned her vitals, Mother hovered toward the ambulance.

"Salutations."

Dash waved. "Salutations."

The admin drone examined her with it's camcorder shaped eyepiece. "Observation: it appears that Dash and the child survived the Crimson Forest despite the probabilities that predicted otherwise."

"Thanks to my trusty sidekick." She pointed at the hoverton. "I owe you one."

The ton titled it's neckpiece. "Suggestion: Annual training slides are still due."

Dash rolled her eyes. "Yes Mother." She shook her head, then stared at the night sky. Stars glimmered through the rain clouds above. "It's funny. When we met the other day, I couldn't wait to go outside and get some action." She squinted, "Secretly I think part of me has always hoped something exciting would happen. But now, I want nothing more than to go back to the safety of my mundane life. I'll take training slides, and computers, and even annoying executives over the dangers of the outside world."

"Query: What about the anomalous code?"

"I did what I set out to do. I found the source and gave the information to Lera. She will get it to the proper authorities. My job is done. It's back to working at the server farms for me. No more adventures for this girl."

Little did Dash know, her journey was just about to begin.

THE END

If you enjoyed this book and would like to get updates on new book releases, lore, artworks and more, check out the Realm Wars Webpage[1]!

---

1. https://www.story-ninjas.com/realmwarsnewsletter

PREVIEW: Realm Wars Episode 2—Reflections of Darkness

Chapter 1

Lera Nightingale scrutinized the holointerface before her. It displayed data from the server farmer's cyber stylus. The resolution wasn't perfect. But she could make out several Daynan symbols. *Crick. Crack. Crick.* Arkery gnawed on something behind her. She turned to the animal. "Hey do you mind? I'm trying to concentrate here." The scaleen cocked it's head, giving a confused look. "Yeah, you." Arkery scooped up his bone then flapped over to the other side of the room. Lera turned her attention back to the holoimage. She rotated the sphere then zoomed in. It was hard to make out all of the glyphs. Several were cracked or worn. But they appeared to all make reference to a term she'd never heard of before. "What's the Navel?" She cross-referenced the information through several interverse repositories. Each query came back with no significant results. The computer couldn't identify any Daynanic references. That was to be expected, though. Out of the thousands of ruins around the galaxy, only a minute number of the artifacts and tablets had been processed or decoded. But it was worth a shot. She would have to dig deeper.

Lera removed the cyber stylus, shutting down the holointerface. Tomorrow, she would have to go out and investigate the ruin herself.

She thought back to her conversation with Dash and Astrea. The child had mentioned an astro-map of some sort. From what the girl described, it sounded like they interacted with the ruin. But how could that be? These new events only raised more questions in Lera's mind. Who exactly was this server farmer? How had she activated the ruins? And what was the Navel?

One thing was certain. The council would need to be notified immediately.

Chapter 2

Inside the lowest levels of an underground facility, an intruder stood surrounded by five sentry-tons. Rhythmic thrumming of alarms wailed through the corridors as the machines approached. Above them, a web of leaky pipes shook like battle drums. *Ba-dum, ba-dum, ba-dum.* Their sole purpose was to prevent unauthorized personnel access to this area. Each one synchronized its movements wirelessly over the ton-net, sending information to the lead unit, U-296. The sentryton's central processor disseminated instructions in near-real-time, which allowed the team to coordinate their attacks in precise unison. Just as the digits on a hand work together to pick up items, so too would each unit work to eliminate the problem.

As they marched toward the infiltrator, U-296 reviewed incoming data. Initial scans provided limited intelligence on the intruder. The target wore black infiltration armor, a helmet, and a cloak. Bioscans came back inconclusive. Probability calculators deduced that microfiber jammers in the suit prevented their sensors from conducting detailed probes. However, based on general height and weight standards the target appeared to be a male organic life-form. There was an 85 percent likelihood that he was a human. Furthermore, incoming security reports supported the assumption that the intruder held responsibility for the deaths of several astro-marines on the upper levels.

The intruder stood in the center of the room, motionless.

U-296 and it's counterparts activated targeting displays as they marched closer.

Systems confirmed that no outside communications had been intercepted, suggesting that the intruder acted alone. Somehow this lone operative slipped through the perimeter defenses and reached the inner chamber. Calculations estimated the probability of this occurrence equaled less than ten percent. Protocol guidelines stated that if an intruder made it this far, then it could be assumed that they were a highly trained professional. Therefore the machines were permitted to use extreme prejudice when performing their duties.

U-296 sent the order to halt. Systems indicated that they had reached optimal attack range.

Its counterparts complied.

Head bowed, the cloaked figure did not move.

Aside from two circular objects attached to the man's shoulder armor, sensors detected nothing out of the ordinary. Scanners flagged them due to their unique metallic composition and shape. They were plate-sized rings made of an unknown material. This obtuse combination warranted a secondary scan for explosive ordinances. Results came back negative. Probability calculators determined they were likely shoulder protection of some sort.

U-296 aimed its weapon at the intruder. In unison, the other machines followed suit. Probability calculations suggested that this would provoke a counter response. However, the intruder made no movements at all. The idea that an organic might freeze when overwhelmed by enemies followed logic.

Tactical files came online.

Behavior patterns dictated that when outnumbered, organics would attempt to flee, but when cornered their tendency was to assume defensive postures. Moreover, sight and sound were the predominant sensory systems for bipedal species. The former was used as a targeting system, while the latter acted as an early warning system. If you degrade an organic's audio receptors, they are more susceptible to visual distractions. Furthermore, unlike machines or synthetics, organics were inefficient at processing large amounts of data, particularly during times of crisis. Rather than addressing problems as a whole, humans approach oncoming issues in the order they occur, leaving them vulnerable to all kinds of manipulations.

Within an instant, the information processed through all five sentry-tons. The attack pattern was transmitted and acknowledged in less than a second.

Step one, block exits by circling the target.

Two, degrade audio receptors with an ultrasonic pulse.

Three, initiate diversion in the form of a frontal attack.

Four, commence secondary attack from the flank.

Five, execution.

Unlike organics, machines were impervious to emotional distractions. However, U-269 preferred the notion that machines could capitalize on human weaknesses in order to achieve their objective. The fact that such frail creatures were the dominant organism in the galaxy continued to perplex the automaton's logic drives.

In perfect unison, the robots surrounded their target.

Head lowered, the intruder stood his ground.

The sentries created an equidistant perimeter around the intruder, then activated hyper-processors, allowing each machine to receive information in slow motion and respond quicker during battle.

In that same second, the machines unleashed an ultrasonic emitter. The tone polluted the airways, intermixing with background noises of blaring alarms and dripping water. The pipes pulsed and the walls wrenched, culminating in a violent flash of energy followed by a sonic boom. Silence swallowed every sound. For a nanosecond, everything stood still. Then the emptiness imploded, unleashing glass, metal, and water at the infiltrator.

The intruder took a knee and used his cloak to deflect the debris. With one elegant sweep of his cape, he effectively shielded his body from the attack.

U-269 replayed the movement and watched in disbelief. Although programs enabled the sentrytons to deal with unorthodox situations, the machines were nonetheless perplexed at the speed and dexterity of this organic. It did not fit within known logic patterns. Nevertheless, they would continue to follow protocol. If the target did not abide by the norms of warfare, they were required to update files for future reference and proceed to the next sequence of the attack.

Head bowed, the infiltrator stood up as if nothing had happened.

Two of U-269's counterparts approached, weapons bearing on the target.

As predicted, the infiltrator crouched into a defensive posture.

The machines fired.

Blam. Blam. Blam.

The target did something not only unexpected but also physically impossible. With lightning speed, the intruder backflipped two meters in the air and evaporated into a mist of darkness, then rematerialized outside of the circle of robots. The infiltrator landed in a crouched position behind them. For approximately half a second, the sentrytons paused to process the new information. This action was not congruent with files on physics. However, probability calculations concluded that the target's ability to perform abnormal acrobatics would not affect their plan of attack or the predicted outcome. Meanwhile, the intruder stood up, flipped his cape back, then detached the rings from his armor and held a disc in each hand.

The machines opened fire again.

Blam. Blam. Blam.

The intruder evaded each attack, flipping and spinning in and out of cover, causing their weapons to reach critical temperatures. In order to prevent overheating, the machines disengaged. It would take approximately three seconds to reach sufficient cooldown, then they could re-engage the target.

Like blood pumping through a vein, lights activated throughout the intruder's suit, glowing magma red from visor to boot. They trickled down the suit.

Vzzt. Vzzt.

The rings illuminated in response.

Audio receptors detected a faint hum emanating from the rim of each circle. The organic spread his arms as if he had wings, sweeping the rings around his body then crouched into a defensive posture, until all four limbs pointed in opposite directions.

Taking the offensive, the attackers fired off two salvos and watched the intruder make a critical mistake. Instead of dodging, he twisted his torso and waved the rings at the fire, in what appeared to be an attempt to block the blazer bolts. Although this was the desired response, for it would result in termination, it was also an illogical course of action, even for an organic. Nothing could block blazer fire. Not even astro-marine armor.

Yet instead of the anticipated fatality, something happened that their processors did not predict. The circular devices caught the blaster fire and absorbed it.

New queries filled U-269's processor. How could the rings consume energy blasts? What sort of technology enabled such a weapon? Would the plan of attack still work, given this new information?

Before systems could predict new probabilities, the infiltrator spun around and redirected the rings toward the sentrytons. The circular beams flashed and a blast of energy blazed through the two closest machines, ripping them to pieces.

Without hesitation, the remaining automatons initiated the next sequence of their strategy: overwhelm the target with attacks from all angles. According to combat theory files, this would force the intruder back into a defensive position. It was unlikely that any organic could withstand a multi-directional assault.

This calculation took a split second to process, then sentrytons commenced the strike and opened fire.

With inhuman precision, the intruder spun his body around, swiping the rings in a figure eight pattern, from left to right and behind the back, connecting with each bolt at the exact moment of impact. A luminous trail followed the wake of his movement and the beams smoldered blood-red.

Slow motion playback showed that the red beams left a mist-like trail. The mist flowed with the movements of the rings, causing a paper-thin energy field to envelop the organic, similar to a force film. Except, the mist could absorb blazer fire.

For the second time in a matter of moments, U-296 found no logical explanation for the organic's ability to defend itself. The ray rings defied several laws of physics. What first appeared to be miscellaneous pieces of armor, were actually highly advanced weapons that could absorb and redirect blazer fire.

Systems updated the device as a weapon, then they re-engaged the intruder with a barrage of their own blazer bolts.

The organic sprung into a backflip, twisting his body 360-degrees. At the apex of the maneuver, he flung his arms out to the sides, releasing the rings. They flew in opposite directions, ricocheting off of the walls and hitting two of U-296's counterparts. *Clank. Clank.* The blows sliced off their headpieces and their bodies crumpled to the floor. The rings boomeranged back to the man, who landed just in time to catch them, then spin around and throw them at U-296 and 297.

Nanoseconds before the circular weapon ended its existence, U-296 witnessed 97 topple to the floor.

Thwack. Thwack.

Warning systems indicated that the ray-ring impaled U-296's thorax compartment. The automaton felt nothing despite the fatal blow. As its chassis collapsed, clanking on the metal floor. U-296 watched the infiltrator raise his arms. Like boomerangs circling back, all four ray rings returned to his hands. He reconnected the devices back to their original configuration and returned them to the shoulder holsters on his armor. Then the infiltrator stalked toward U-296 and bent down. As critical systems failed, the sentry-ton stared at its executioner. The man removed his helmet, revealing an unexpected sight. The intruder was not human at all. Nor was it cybotic, or synthetic.

But it did match one organic species.

But that is illogical.

As the last trails of calculation evaporated into oblivion, confusion struck the machine. The information it received must have been corrupted because it was not logical.

The face staring back at U-269 did belong to a human. Rather it belonged to a long extinct race that, until this moment, were believed to be nothing more than a religious fable.

The Vishnigh.

Chapter 3

The intruder who just moments earlier stood outnumbered five-to-one bent over the last sentryton's remains. He watched intently as its optical receptors flickered out of existence.

The infiltrator removed the machine's head plate and inspected it. The unit designator read *U-296.*

He imagined what the robot would do if it had a soul. What would it do with consciousness? Would it attempt to rid itself from this physical prison and escape its wretched existence? No longer restrained to its programming, would it choose to be something else? No longer a slave, would it choose to be someone else?

A spaceship perhaps, sailing the stars?

No, a ship is still a machine. It would want to be something living, like an animal.

Perhaps a bird?

Yes, yes. A bird.

A dove ascending to heaven, becoming one with the realms above. It would soar above all life's problems. Untouchable. No longer trapped by rules and regulations. Finally able to think on its own. Finally able to dream on its own. Free to live life however it saw fit.

The cloaked figure smiled. What a wish.

For the first time in its existence, the robot would feel something. It would experience emotions; happiness, sadness, fear, anger, and maybe even love. Perhaps one day it would even have a family of its own. He imagined a mother dove bringing food back to the nest and feeding its baby chicks.

How innocent youth was.

And defenseless...

The intruder dropped the machine's headpiece to the floor.

Clank.

Youth was also fragile and naive; easy for predators to take advantage of. He imagined how simple it would be for a snake to gobble up each little chick one by one.

A message blinked on the holocom distracting him from his thoughts.

He answered it. An insect looking alien stared back through the three-dimensional display.

Tic-tu-da-tuck-nic.

The Collective commander spoke in its native language and the phonic system translated.

"Reeve Daychron-Urn, her majesty requests an audience."

Daychron surveyed the area. A pair of double doors stood along the adjacent wall, decorated with Daynanic art. The artifact he came for was just beyond those doors.

"I'm just finishing up here."

"Acknowledged." The commander clicked. "A beacon was activated."

Daychron snapped his attention back to the holo-display. "A beacon?"

The creature's wings fluttered. Daychron wasn't great at deciphering alien body language, but he was pretty sure that the fluttering gesture meant agreement.

"Inform her highness that I will contact her immediately."

The reeve deactivated his holo-com and glared back at the sentry-ton.

Perhaps it's better that the machine didn't have a soul. To have a soul gives one the capacity to care. And caring only leads to tragedy. Better to be soulless than to go through the world vulnerable. When you have nothing to lose, you are strong. Predators do not hunt the strong. They *are* the strong.

He strode toward the doors.

Like the machine, he had no soul. It had been stolen from him long ago, gobbled up by a snake that took advantage of his good nature.

And all that mattered now was preventing that serpent from coming back.

All that mattered were the gateways.

Chapter 4

The lights dimmed as Reeve Daychron entered his personal prowler-craft, *The Spectre*. He activated the quantum encrypted holo-com and placed his hand over the device. After conducting a bioscan, it blinked green. The transmission started and a masked figure appeared on the holo-display.

His master, Alexian.

Reeve Daychron knelt. "Your majesty. What is thy command?"

"An obelisk has been activated," she said.

Even after all of these years, that modulated voice still made him uneasy. However, the information she just disclosed gave him chills.

"Activated?"

"In the Frontier Sector, on a planet called Hestia." His master nodded to another shadowy figure. Daychron could only distinguish the person's silhouette. But there was no mistaking the priestlike headdress they wore. A holographic map of Conglomerate space appeared. A solitary dot blinked like a beacon. Daychron furrowed his brow. The beacons were disabled centuries when the galactic gateways were destroyed. Unless this belonged to a realmic window? But who could have activated it? The Vasilikaim were all wiped out during the Great Purge. His master was all that remained of that ancient bloodline.

"Gather your wraith brethren and investigate the area."

Daychron bowed his head. "As you command, your Highness."

Chapter 5

Pat.

Pat.

Pat.

A constant drizzle fell on the ruins as salvage-tons cleared the area of debris. Beyond them, a team of highly trained security personnel scouted the perimeter around the lake. Lera was grateful for their presence, as they were the only deterrent against the bush people. If she was right, this site might be the key to unlocking the gateways. The Daynanic Empire was the oldest in recorded history. Almost every myth from around the galaxy referenced them in some manner, shape, or form. It dated so far back that even ancient civilizations referenced the Daynan as prehistoric. Yet, they clearly had more advanced technology than even the most cutting-edge modern equipment in existence, which allowed them to colonize the known galaxy. Some even believed they were capable of extragalactic travel. Others claimed that such feets were hyperbolic exaggerations stemming from fairy tales and legends.

"She will need to be monitored."

"A server farmer? Dranco, you can't be serious."

"What other leads do we have?"

"So you think she's one of *them*?"

"You said she has a techno tattoo, right? Until we know for certain, we can't rule it out."

"Please, Director Soren practically raised this girl."

"Lera, you know as well as I do that the council will want a report. You'll need to keep an eye on her."

"Do you really think that's necessary?"

"HQ lost contact with an entire astro-marine platoon at the Brutan facility moments after that obelisk was activated. It can't be a coincidence. If these incidents are connected, we must find out."

"Do they really think it's cybots?"

"That's what they sent me to investigate. But we're in Frontier space, who else could it be?"

Lera nodded and disconnected the secure holocom. Things just got much more complicated.

Chapter 6

As Dash ascended the stairs to her personal quarters, her muscles protested against each step. She struggled to open the screen door to her personal quarters. Her shoulder still throbbed from the scuffle in the Crimson Forest. Dash hated to admit it but she had never been so happy to be home. All she wanted to do was curl up in bed and go to sleep. As she passed through the entryway, the lights flickered to life. Dash raised a hand, blocking her eyes. "Deluminate by fifty percent." The lights dimmed to a more manageable level. Once her eyes adjusted to the light, she removed her virtual vizard and tossed it in the trash can. A lot of good that was now. After the explosion at the ruins, the company mask was more useless than a remote control with no batteries. Dash scanned her trailer and sighed. A pile of dishes sat in the sink while a mountain of clothes lay on the floor. She pointed at the mess. "*You* are future me's problem."

Right now, it was time to relax.

Dash rubbed the back of her neck, glad that the day was over. "Time to take off the armor," she said, unfastening her utility cuff. As she peeled away each piece of her enviro-suit, she could feel her body relax more and more. The holocom chimed, breaking her train of thought. It was a reminder. Tomorrow was Soren's trifecta file-day. She shook her head and removed her boots. "That old geezer, I can't believe he's turning 111. I'll have to give him a call."

Once she got down to her undergear, Dash trudged to her bathroom and grabbed her toothbrush. As she opened the cabinet to get the toothpaste, she caught a glimpse of her reflection in the mirror.

She dropped the toothbrush and her body froze. Dash wasn't in her trailer. She was back at the ruins, hand stuck in the aqua-interface.

Pain surged through Dash's body as a series of images raced through her mind.

A giant centipede monster emerged from a cave.

Flash.

A glowing pebble.

Flash.

Droves of insectoid cyborgs attacked the Hestia colony.

Flash.

The glowing pebble, laying on the ground.

Flash.

A woman wearing a black mask that covered half of her face, stared back at her.

Flash.

The glowing pebble again. Dash felt compelled to pick it up.

Flash.

Corpses of colonists lay intermingled with the husks of insectoid aliens.

Flash.

The pebble. She could hear it calling to her.

Dash.

The masked woman. She was saying something. No. Yelling something. Was the woman calling her name? No. It was Astrea. And she was screaming. The shrieks reeled Dash back to reality. Galaxies and stars swirled about her mind like a whirlpool until the vision blipped out of existence. Her bathroom mirror came back into focus, along with her reflection.

Dash's head ached and her stomach felt woozy. What just happened? Had she been brushing her teeth? Or, going to the bathroom? She couldn't quite recall. Dash forced herself to her room and laid down on the bed. As she pulled the covers over her body, it continued to nag at her. What had she forgotten? And another, less important question—did the team raid *Sins of the Serpent* without her? Dash noticed messages on her holocom but felt too exhausted to check them. Had Ave tried to call? No, that made no sense. Every second felt like an eternity. Nauseousness overtook her body, and before she knew it dark spots filled her periphery.

Want to know when Reflections Of Darkness: Realm Wars Book 2 goes live? Sign up to the mailing list![2]

---

2.   https://bookhip.com/JTLABZG

Other Books By Josh Coker

Steampunk Wars: Beyond The Rim Preview

Chapter 1

Anna Windrider sat in the captain's chair of the *Evangeline*, revolver in hand. After inspecting the barrel, she flicked the cylinder into place, then rolled it across her sleeve. Each chamber clicked as the mechanism rotated. The weapon comforted her. The smoothness of the handle reassured her. In some ways, the pistol was the only thing that made sense anymore. She locked the hammer back into position and looked around the room. Various dials and gauges surrounded her. Each one lifeless, much like the ship itself. Anna used to consider this place home.

But how could anywhere be safe?

Not now.

Not after what she had seen.

She pushed the image from her mind and inhaled another draw of her pipe. The opium only dulled the memories. It did not erase them. Anna could still hear the laborer's screams. They echoed in her mind and she gripped the gun tighter.

That damned explorer.

She shouldn't have taken the job.

If only she'd listened to her gut.

If only.

A board creaked. Anna spun around, gun raised. Her index finger hovered over the trigger. But she saw nothing. Instead, her reflection glared back at her through the glass. The visage that stared back, a mere shadow of her former self. Disheveled hair. Pale skin. Tattered clothes. She shuddered, and exhaled. As she slumped back into the captain's chair, tears slid down her cheeks.

Madness threatened to take hold of her mind.

Nothing made sense anymore.

Nothing was right.

Only a month ago the world represented a place of opportunity and adventure.

But now?

Why had she taken that job?

She shook her head.

"Fool," she said out loud, then pressed the barrel to her temple.

Chapter 2

If Anna had to pick one place in the entire Empire to call home, it would be the Air Harbors.

Vast bodies of dirigibles and airships filled the docks. Engines roared as they came and went. The aromas of food mixed with engine exhaust, giving the wharf a smell of bacon and oil. Droves of citizens from every walk of life and every corner of the Empire came here to do business.

To Anna, the harbors represented a place of opportunity and adventure.

She sat at the base of the boarding ramp, boots propped up on a folding table. Behind her, the *Evangeline* hovered. The cables that held the airship to the dock sang in the breeze. Its domed gas envelope provided shade against the afternoon sun. Before her, Anna watched the harbor go about its business. Vendors held trays of food in front of passersby. A retailer hawked his wares. Strange creatures from some far-flung part of the world. He claimed they gave blessings of good luck. On the other side of the dock, a captain haggled over fuel prices. Further down she could see local girls trying to sweet talk a bunch of sailors.

Anna shook her head. *Everyone does business here.*

Normally she enjoyed her time at the harbors. But weeks had passed since their last job. If that's what you called it. At first, the crew jumped at a chance for shore leave. But now, relaxation turned to restlessness, and restlessness turned to boredom. She already lost one crew member to a rival captain offering better pay. Armin and Kristoff were at each other's throats. And Jen would probably quit if she didn't get any coin soon.

Her crew needed a job.

Anna tapped her boot against the table.

A large cargo shipment sat near their mooring point. It arrived earlier this morning. Normally that was a good sign. But the shipment came with no manifesto. No instructions for delivery. No message, or even anything to identify who it belonged to.

It was just, *there*.

Taking up space.

Space in front of her ship.

Space that could be given to cargo they could actually transport.

She glared at the crates as if she could melt them with her eyes. Hour after hour went by and they continued sitting there, refusing to declare their intent. Reaching into her jacket, Anna retrieved a pocket watch and checked the time. Her first mate, Armin, should have been back by now. She'd sent him to solve the cargo mystery hours ago. How long did it take to get a name? Maybe he stopped for some local cuisine, she speculated. While it wasn't like Armin to meander, he had quite an appetite for exotic foods. Another thought popped in her mind. Perhaps it was military equipment? If that was the case, Armin probably had to deal with a dock official, which meant it could take all day.

She rolled her eyes.

Great.

Anna tucked the watch back into her pocket, removed her gloves, and set to picking her nails with a small boot knife.

"Captain Windrider, I presume?" someone asked.

She didn't recognize the voice, but it sounded like money.

Anna craned her neck to get a better look at the stranger.

An older man approached.

"That depends," she replied, slipping the knife beneath her ruffled sleeve. "Who's asking?"

While the question seemed innocent enough, not many customers came looking for her by name.

The gentleman stopped at her table. Golden gears decorated his top-hat and adorned his duck-tailed suit. He held a cane in his hand. The handle was a dragon's head. To Anna, the man looked like a stick bug dressed in an expensive suit. "I beg your pardon," the man said. He removed his top hat and bowed. Silver hairs danced in the breeze. "Sir Earnest Walmsley, at your service." Excitement jolted through Anna's body and she sat up straight. If memory served her correctly, Earnest Walmsley was the explorer that found the lost city of Atlantis. So, if the gentleman was who he claimed to be, then he definitely had money. And she definitely wanted his business.

Anna tried to act nonchalant. "Walmsley? Sounds familiar."

He chuckled, then realized Anna wasn't joking.

The old man leaned in and whispered, "Atlantis."

"Oh, right. Atlantis." She snapped her fingers. "You're that explorer," Anna said, attempting to remain stony. If Walmsley sensed nervousness, then he would have the upper hand in negotiations.

"Indeed." He adjusted his bowtie. "Although I try not to take the credit. I was merely the instigator of the expedition. My crew and fellow explorers found the lost city."

"Is that so?"

The man nodded.

Anna's father tracked the Atlantis expedition with great interest when she was a child. She recalled newspaper articles and wireless broadcasts about the discovery. For someone who didn't want to claim the credit for Atlantis, Mr. Walmsley spent an awful lot of time speaking to the press.

"So, Mister Walms—"

"Earnest. Please, Captain, call me Earnest." He smiled.

"Earnest, then. What can I do for you?" she asked. The fact that she was speaking face-to-face with her father's idol felt surreal. "You've already discovered Atlantis. You have a fleet of airships from what I understand. What do you need from me? My crew doesn't take illegal jobs, if that's what this is about."

He chuckled.

"Illegal? Oh heavens no! Quite the opposite in fact. I want your crew because I'm reliably informed that you're one of the few captains who will go beyond the Rim."

Anna's eyes narrowed.

That information wasn't widely known.

"You were informed correctly sir, but it's not something we do often." She gave him a sideways look. "Or cheaply, for that matter."

He waved the idea away as though it meant nothing.

"Money won't be a problem," he said.

Anna supposed that, to him, it probably wasn't.

He reached inside his overcoat and produced a scroll of paper. With a flourish, he unrolled it on the table. "It took me some time, and considerable effort, to find this map," he said.

Anna glanced over the document. It was an aeronautical map, not much different from the one her navigator used. If something special lay hidden in its charts, Anna couldn't find it.

"What's so special about this map?"

"It shows something that no other map in the world does."

"And what's that?"

The old man removed a monocle from his vest and placed it over his eye. "This," he said, tapping the northern part of the map.

Anna followed his finger. Her eyes went wide when she saw what he pointed at. The dot indicated a city far north of the Rim. Most other maps marked this area as unexplored territory, so she hadn't bothered to look there. Upon further inspection, she noticed more details. Other landmarks filled the area beyond the Rim. Supposed islands and continents.

"A city?" she asked, still reviewing the map.

"Indeed," Earnest said. He raised a finger, "but not just any city. It has no name. At least not one that's recorded in any history book. According to Atlantean legends, the gods built a temple here. And I believe a forgotten treasure lies within."

Treasure.

Excitement surged through Anna's body. "What kind of treasure."

"Forgotten secrets." He gazed into the distance. "Secrets that explain the technology of the Ancients."

Many explorers from across the Empire dreamed of unlocking the mysteries of the Ancients. While many ruins and artifacts remained, not much was known about the Ancients themselves. Somehow they constructed the most sophisticated structures on the planet. And yet, no one knew what they were used for. Moreover, they seemed to have disappeared suddenly, and without a trace. Scientists gave theories of course. Most revolved around crystal technology and portals. Others suggested aliens from outer space. For years, many academics, including Anna's father, believed Atlantis held the answers. But after decades of excavation, nothing significant turned up. Personally, Anna didn't have the luxury of caring about such theories. Her concerns were far more immediate. But, whether the old man was right or not, a lost city beyond the Rim would be quite a find. Teaming up with Walmsley on an excursion this important would surely boost her reputation in certain circles, which in turn would help with future employment.

But a temple of the gods?

In her experience, so-called gods tended to be tall tails meant to scare children, or in this case, seduce explorers. They normally turned out to be disgruntled creatures or pirates looking for a ransom. Anna would rather not tangle with either. She may be desperate for coin, but not that desperate. She rolled up the map, and handed it back to the old man. "The Hunting Corps is further down the dock, sir."

"You asked me what I wanted, Captain." Earnest drew himself up to his full, dignified height. "I want to find this city and claim it for the Empire. I want to be first. And I want you and your crew to help me do it."

Anna considered the man for a long moment. His face could barely conceal his excitement. Whether the city actually existed or not, he believed every word he spoke. But, given the fact that he *was* the founder of Atlantis, his story held more credence than most.

"Have you ever been outside the Rim, my lord?"

"I must admit, I have not. As you know, Atlantis sits within its borders. What, if I might ask, was your experience of it?"

"Fascinating and terrifying, in equal measure."

She studied his reaction carefully.

When he merely nodded, she decided that the venture might be worth pursuing. At least he seemed to respect the danger of the world beyond the Rim.

"We may be able to help. But, as I mentioned earlier, we don't go beyond the Rim cheaply. I know you said money won't be a problem but..." she left the last part of the sentence unspoken, allowing the subtext to hang in the air.

"Name a price."

Anna responded instantly. The number she gave had been in her mind ever since he mentioned the Rim. The price was extortionate, even for what he was asking. But she wanted to see just how deep his pockets were.

"Done," he said, clapping his hands together.

He extended his arm for a handshake to seal the deal. "Captain, you won't regret this."

Anna shook his hand while replaying the answer in her head. The man agreed to her price without a second thought. She stared at him, somewhat dazed from the unexpected response. She imagined all of the things she could buy with the money. They could fix the engines. Hell, they could buy brand new engines. They could finally get the shell resprayed. They could stock the kitchen with proper food and supplies. Hire a full crew. She could even pay off Fist, and get his goons off her back.

What he offered was more than a small fortune. It was freedom for Anna and her crew. After a moment, she realized that Earnest was still talking and pulled herself back to reality.

"I'm sorry, could you repeat that?" she asked.

"Can we start loading onto the ship? I do wish to make good time, after all, Captain."

"Loading?" she asked.

Earnest gestured toward the group of men behind him. They carried the mystery pile of cargo from earlier.

She eyed Earnest. "*You?*"

"I like to be prepared, Captain. My apologies if I have overstepped my bounds." He bowed, then turned to direct his men.

Anna stood incredulous, as new questions filled her mind.

Who exactly was Earnest Walmsley, and how the hell would convince her crew to go beyond the Rim?

Chapter 3

Anna approached the bridge, ready to brief her crew on the details of the job. The aromas of nicotine and licorice filled the air. She knew the smell originated from Jen's cigar. While the mechanic didn't smoke them, she chewed on them like a dog with a bone. As she walked through the doorway, the beastly woman greeted her with a grunt. Grease stains smattered her overalls. Anna nodded back. While Jen may have lacked the appearance of a lady, she more than made up for it with her skills as a mechanic. The woman's ingenuity had saved their skins more than once. The first mate, Armin, sat in the corner, sharpening his scimitar. The blade grated against the whetstone with each pass he made. The exotic man's lean musculature and relaxed demeanor was that of a cat. Kristoff, the navigator, waddled about the room, reading what appeared to be another novel. When he noticed Anna, the young man closed the book.

"Hey Cap."

"Kristoff."

"What's going on with the visitors? New job?"

Anna handed him Earnest's map.

He opened it and spread it across the navigation table. As Kristoff pored over the document, Jen leaned in closer. Armin continued to scrape his sword, as if oblivious to the conversation.

"Our client is leading an expedition."

"Finally, we're leaving this hellhole," Jen said.

"What's the destination?" Kristoff asked.

Anna pointed to the landmark on the map.

The navigator's eyes widened.

"You're kidding, right?"

Jen peered over his shoulder. "What is it?"

Kristoff looked to Armin. "Do you see this?"

The first mate just kept on sharpening his blade.

Anna held her hands up. She had anticipated pushback. No one, including herself, *wanted* to go beyond the Rim. "Just calm down."

"Calm down?" Kristoff asked, incredulous. "To hell with that." He pointed a finger out the viewport. "Do you have any idea how many ships have been lost at the edge of the Rim this past year?"

Anna crossed her arms.

Kristoff looked across the room at the others.

"Almost twenty. And they didn't even go beyond it."

She shook her head. He may be the best damn navigator in the Empire, but the kid had no taste for adventure.

"It's not like we've never been beyond the Rim before," Armin said, eyes never leaving his blade.

"So what if we've been out there before?" This time it was Jen who chimed in. She took the cigar out of her mouth and gestured toward the starboard section of the ship where new defensive plating covered the hull. "I don't recall that going well either."

"Really? You're going to bring that up?" Kristoff huffed.

"You're not the one who spent a month fixing the damn thing."

"Maybe if the engines had held up, I wouldn't have been forced to make that maneuver."

The mechanic's jaw clenched, as did her fist.

Armin looked up. "We are wiser now."

"Wiser?" Jen scoffed. She looked to Anna. "Frontz left. We have no surgeon. But we're taking a job beyond the Rim?"

She had a point. Going beyond the Rim without a medic was not the best idea ever. But there was no time to find a doctor now. Between the four of them, Anna felt confident the crew had enough experience to handle most bumps and bruises. "Once we finish this job, we can afford to hire more personnel," Anna said.

"I swear to God, Captain, I'm finding another ship."

"Like we haven't heard that before," Kristoff said.

Jen's eyes narrowed. "Pipe down powderboy."

Kristoff pursed his lips.

The bear of a woman turned back to Anna. "We better be getting paid this time, Captain."

"Oh, we're getting paid," Anna said. She let the silence hang for a minute to add weight to her words.

Jen looked to Armin, probably expecting him to fill her in.

The first mate just kept sharpening his sword.

"How much?" Kristoff asked, unable to contain the anxiety in his voice.

Anna told them the contract amount.

"Well grind my gears."

Jen's mouth opened so wide, Anna thought the cigar might fall right out of her mouth.

Kristoff looked as though he'd just been punched in the gut. "That changes things." He inched back into the navigator's chair, then reexamined the map. "If these nav charts are accurate, it should take about a month to reach the destination."

For the first time since the conversation began, the grinding noise stopped. Armin stood up and sheathed his sword. He looked around at the group. "Looks like we have work to do."

"I'll go give the engines a once over." Jen stuffed the cigar back in her mouth and strode out of the room without another word.

After that, they gathered supplies for the journey and made sure the *Evangeline* was airworthy before they took off. It wouldn't do to fall out of the sky before they even got past the harbors. As they prepared to make way, Anna could only hope that she was making the right decision for herself, and her crew.

The Hunt

Chapter 1

I scrolled through my phone the whole drive up, not really looking for anything in particular. Couple cute girls from school. A funny meme. The usual. I couldn't help myself. Pops sat in the driver's seat, going on and on about his last hunt.

"This year, I'm gonna get the bastard," he said.

The radio blared country music, breaking my concentration. Pops patted his hands against the steering wheel to the beat.

Ugh. Spare me.

Before we left, Mom gave me the "Pops won't be here forever" speech. I rolled my eyes. If Pops was an animal, he'd be a reptile. Not only was he cold-blooded, he'd probably outlive us all.

Pops glared at my phone.

"Enjoy it while it lasts," he said. "When we get to camp, that's going in the glove box."

"But Pops."

He raised an eyebrow.

Better not argue or he'll take it away now.

We spent the rest of the ride in silence. Pops listened to country music. I watched videos on my phone.

We arrived at camp around dusk.

Pops got a fire going.

"Go ahead and set up the tent. If you get stuck, the instructions are under the flap."

Set up the tent? What a crock.

I examined the instructions.

While they may have existed two decades ago, years of rainstorms must have faded the directions. So much so that now they resembled more of a cryptic treasure map, than actual words. *If I had my phone, I could just look up a video on how to assemble the tent.* Instead, I struggled to figure it out for nearly an hour. Rentable cabins stood just across the dirt path. Cabins with walls. Walls that prevented bugs, snakes, and bears from coming in. Cabins that had air conditioning and heaters. Cabins that had beds.

Must be nice.

"Cabin would have been easier."

Pops scoffed. "Grab some beans, and I'll help you finish up later."

I didn't tell him I hated beans. He already seemed disappointed about the cabin comment. Sometimes I wondered how we could even be related. I mean, not only was he into outdoorsy stuff, but he always wore those stupid trucker hats.

I took some crackers and mixed them with the beans.

"First hunt. You excited?" he asked.

Not really. But I know you don't want to hear that.

"Of course."

I choked down a bite of my food.

"Got the perfect spot this year. Treestand's all set up. Just you wait. Finally get to use those skills from the hunter's ed course."

I pursed my lips.

Don't remind me. I'd rather not relive the shooting-range fiasco. So humiliating.

"Guess so."

Pops pointed a spoon full of beans at me. "Back in the day, men killed what they ate. Hunt it, shoot it, skin it, cook it, eat it."

Images flashed through my mind.

I gagged.

Skinning and eating animals? Suddenly my appetite disappeared.

Pops waved a dismissive hand.

"You kids," he said.

Great, here we go. Life lesson mode.

"Don't have any connection to nature. Don't know why you're alive, or how to keep yourselves that way. You just..."

His words trailed off and he looked up. A man with an eyepatch stood at our fire. He wore a faded flannel shirt and mud-stained jeans. Flashlights adorned his utility belt. His unkempt demeanor and boney features resembled that of a vulture.

"Well if it ain't Old Bloodhound," the man said.

Pops nodded.

The visitor took a swig of his beer. "And this must be the young pup." His single eye scanned me from head to toe. "Here to get lessons from the 'Greatest Tracker in the South,' are we?"

Is he talking about Pops?

I didn't know what to say.

He scoffed.

Pops eyed me. "Jason, this is Pete," he said. "One of the oldest hunters in camp."

The weather-worn man shot a glance at Pops. "You tell him yet?"

Pops ignored the question. Instead he gazed into the campfire, then grabbed a stick and poked a log. The flame flared and I could feel the heat on my face.

"Leave the past in the past."

"Did you tell him?" Pete demanded.

Pops looked at me and sighed. "I will."

Pete grunted, tipped his hat, then hobbled toward the other side of camp.

Once the haggard man passed beyond earshot, I leaned in.

"What was that all about?"

Pops pursed his lips. "Nothing."

I cocked my head. "Nothing? Come on. What was he talking about?"

Pops sighed.

"Back when Uncle Frank was about your age, a group of us used to go out hunting. Pete, his brother, couple other guys." He squinted. "Must be going on twenty years now. One day Pete came over the walkie-talkie screaming and hollering. By the time we got to him, his brother was gone."

Gone?

Wait, like dead?

"Gone? What do you mean?"

Pops shrugged. "Just gone. Pete was covered in blood and Dan was nowhere to be found. Said a monster attacked them."

My eyes went wide.

"A monster?"

Pops frowned. "Probably just a bear. Don't you worry much about it. The rangers never found any evidence. Ever since then, they call him Crazy Pete. If you ask me, he just couldn't get past it. Witnessing the death of a loved one can be a traumatic experience."

I cocked an eyebrow.

Wait a minute.

A monster?

Bears?

Yeah right.

Pops and the veterans must tell this story to all of the new hunters. *Some sort of a scare tactic. A hazing ritual they put all the young guys through.*

Well I'm not falling for it.

I smirked. "You're just trying to scare me."

Pops didn't reply.

He just stared back into the fire, brooding.

Chapter 2

The restroom sat on the other side of camp. And thank goodness it did. The smell made me gag. It barely qualified as a porta-potty, never mind a bathroom. *Still, it's better than going in the woods.* I trekked back to the campsite. Wildlife surrounded me. Crickets chirped. Frogs croaked. Owls hooted. Life was all around. *Not like the city.* Here, everything fit together.

Maybe Pops was onto something. The forest held a sort of timeless charm. While camping definitely wasn't my thing, I could see why the old man found it so alluring. It was primal.

Just like Pops.

Laughter broke my train of thought.

A group of hunters gathered around a campfire. Crazy Pete stood in the center.

"The smell," he said flaring his nostrils, "like a rotten carcass."

I moved in closer so I could hear the rest of his story.

"...footprints as big as a tree stump," Pete continued.

A guy that looked like a hog wearing a flannel shirt interrupted. "You scared Bigfoot with a flashlight? Yeah right."

A woman sat next to the burly man. She tugged at his shirt. "Honey, let him finish."

The fat man waved his hand in dismissal. "I suppose it has red glowing eyes too? I heard the same story at the reservation last year." He chugged the remainder of his beer. "Except, the Indians said it was a demon that hibernated for decades at a time." The man stood up and looked at the group. "He probably got it off of a website or something." He wiped his face, then left the group. The woman reluctantly followed.

After that, the story's spell wore off.

Everyone around the campfire dispersed.

"Remember, don't stay out past dusk. It's nocturnal," Crazy Pete called out.

Pete looked back at me and I caught his eye for a second. He limped over. *I should go.*

"Your grandfather don't believe me neither. Never has," he said. "But you're smarter than that. You smell like a book." He raised his finger. "Listen, Old Bloodhound might be able to track an ant through a rainstorm, but he can't find something he ain't looking for. Just don't stay out after dark."

I nodded my head. Pete turned and left.

I returned to the tent. Pops snored. *Old man fell asleep quick.* I slipped into the tent and closed my eyes. Finding a comfortable position proved difficult. Every time I switched positions a rock poked me, or a stick jabbed me.

"Stop fidgeting," Pops mumbled.

I stared at the roof of the tent. It rippled in the wind, casting eerie shadows like long, skeletal fingers on the fabric. Leaves rustled and insects skittered about. The wind changed directions and blew campfire smoke into the tent. A pine odor assaulted my nostrils.

"Hey Pops," I said.

He grunted.

"Is Pete really crazy?"

Pops just kept snoring.

Chapter 3

For a long while I lay there, restless. I missed my room. What I wouldn't give to have my comfy bed, with its soft pillows and cozy blankets. Or at least a blanket, that actually covered my entire body. No doubt, my buddies were playing Warzone. *Which is what I should be doing.* Instead, I was stuck here, in the armpit of nowhere. The whole crew would be online this weekend. Multiplayer would be giving bonus points, meaning they would level twice as fast. It would take me at least a week to catch up. Until then, no one would want me on the team. My character would be too weak to keep up.

Why did my parents have to go out of town this weekend? This is so frustrating. I can't fall asleep. I can't eat real food. I can't message my friends. I can't find out who's on the leaderboards. This is maddening. If only I had my phone... I glanced over at Pops. The old man snored, his chest rising and falling with each breath. *I bet I could grab the phone out of the truck. But, if I get caught, I won't see my phone for the rest of the week. Too risky.*

I closed my eyes. Images of Warzone flashed through my mind.

Damn it. I have to know.

I slipped out of my sleeping bag and snuck through the tent flap. I stepped outside and snuck in the truck. I opened the glove box and stole my phone.

I clicked the top button and activated the device. The screen displayed zero bars. No cellular reception.

Of course. This is so not fair.

Still, a few updates and messages awaited me. They must have come through before Pops took the phone. My buddies posted pictures at the game store. Waiting lines snaked outside the store entrance and wrapped around the next building. I saw all my buddies. John, Ray, Chris, and Anna. Man, she looked so hot in that new shirt. Richie already bought the game and uploaded pictures of his new character. I couldn't wait to make my own. I switched off my phone. No doubt, more updates would come in the morning.

If I took the phone with me, reception might be better on the trail tomorrow. However, if Pops caught me, I'd be dead for sure.

I held the phone in my hand and chewed my lip. *What to do, what to do?* Pops may not always be easy to get along with, but I did love him. And I didn't want to disrespect him. Once we got to the treestand, I'd probably be bored out of my mind. Sitting for hours staring at trees and grass didn't fall on the list of top ten things I always wanted to do. *I should just bring it. Tomorrow I can put the phone back in the truck.*

Pops would never know.

I tucked the phone in my cargo pocket and went back to bed. After a few more minutes, I fell fast asleep.

About The Author

Josh is a military veteran, public speaker, and father of three. Josh has published multiple science fiction, fantasy and nonfiction books. When not writing, Josh plays video games like Mass Effect, God of War and Mortal Kombat. Growing up as a comic book geek in the 80's, Josh has an affinity for superhero stories. He's also a huge fan of classic Star Wars and owns multiple lightsabers. His other hobbies include powerlifting, roller skating, and beach bumming.

You can learn more about Josh by checking out his Youtube channel, or his blog. Feel free to follow Josh on social media, to get updates on all of his latest projects.

E-mail: jcoker@story-ninjas.com
Instagram: @Joshumusprime[1]
Facebook: Josh Coker[2]
YouTube: @Tipperdy[3]

---

1. https://www.instagram.com/joshumusprime/?hl=en

2. https://www.facebook.com/thepolymathparadigm/

3. https://www.youtube.com/channel/UCL0CQjXGVCaf6vyRfOyAQRQ

Thank You From Story Ninjas

Story Ninjas Publishing would like to thank you for reading this story. We hope you found value in our book and would love to hear your feedback. Please provide your constructive criticism in a review on Amazon. Also feel free to share this book with your friends through various social media platforms.

Other Books by Story Ninjas
Story Ninjas Publishing hopes you enjoyed this book. Check out our website for more products you may be interested in.

League Of Assassins: Betrayal Preview

Chapter 1

Year 1520 of the Fourth Astra Reign

The rain fell for months in the region and the forests were thick and lush because of it. From deep within the canyons of the White Lions Mountain range, the war drums of the Sky Castle announced the movement of the Astra Knight army. The realm was deeply entrenched in a savage war between forces of the Light and forces of the Dark. The Astra King's grip on the realm slowly began to slip, for the Shadow spread down from the North and so the tension mounted. The High Mountain Road ran deep into the White Lions Mountains, and it acted as the only true route of transportation through the treacherous hills. Astra Knights were seen day and night as they patrolled and conducted security checks to protect the region from intruders, especially in such dangerous times. Often seen in the distance were their torches, and if those were not in sight, one only had to look hard for the bright gleam of their Astra Blades. Blades made from the hardest and most powerful element in the entire realm. Even through the darkest of shadows, Ether Glass would light the way.

A hooded figure emerged from the forest. He walked slowly and with purpose, as he followed the Astra Knights from a distance, eyeing them.

Stalking them, hunting them.

Each step sank into the Earth under his immense weight and when he stood tall, his height reached well over seven feet.

A long black cape trailed behind him and rustled silently in the wind; it appeared to meld into the shadows, giving it the semblance that it was endless. Giant strides brought him closer and closer to the unsuspecting soldiers and yet they could not hear or sense him. He moved like a shadow, he was a shadow, seemingly catlike in his agility, and he found himself within arm's reach in a matter of seconds. From beneath his cloak, his hand emerged, in his palm hovered a black orb of energy that throbbed with the intensity of a dying star. In one motion he swept his arm across the backside of four Astra Knights and sent them flying into the forest like they were children's dolls. Before the other Knights realized what had happened, the man turned to them and drew his other hand out. As he did, the ball of black energy formed into a long jagged black blade, six feet in length that sliced through their armor and flesh, discerning no difference between the two. The Astra Knights crumpled into pieces, their wounds sizzled and smoked, and were charred black as night. The Shadow Titan smirked beneath his hood, and returned his hands beneath his cloak as he marched on down the road.

"Halt! Stop right there sir, show your face." Two armed Astra Knights stood determined a hundred yards away.

The Shadow Titan lowered his gaze, and moved on without looking up at them.

"Sir, you are trespassing on the land of the Astra King, ruler of the Sky Kingdom and the White Lions Mountain region. As an Astra Knight of the King's first regiment, I order you to stop where you are this instant."

The Shadow Titan stopped dead in his tracks and slowly raised his gaze. A deep guttural laugh emerged from beneath his hood. The Astra Knights drew their swords, baffled looks on their faces made it seem like they were unsure of what else they could do.

"Remove your hood or we will be forced to attack you sir, and we will not hold back if you continue to disobey our orders." The Astra Knight on the left stepped forward, and kept his sword pointed toward the Shadow Titan. His partner on the right stood behind him with a nervous look on his face.

The Shadow Titan stepped forward, now within striking distance of the two Knights. He turned his head and stared only at the Knight in the rear, as he ignored the knight directly in front of him. For a brief second a cloud of darkness fell over the Knight's eyes.

"Do not make another move, or I will be forced to—" The Knight's body dropped to the ground, blood sprayed from his neck and his head rolled down past the Shadow Titan's feet and settled onto the side of the road in a shallow mud puddle. The other Knight fell to his knees, a look of disbelief on his face, clutching his sword that dripped with his partner's blood. A look of horror on his face as he stared in shock at his blade, then slowly looked up at the Shadow Titan, who had remained perfectly still and silent as far as the Astra Knight could tell, this entire time.

"How?" was all he managed to sputter before the man of darkness leaped into the air, his Shadow Blade emerging from beneath his cloak.

All was silent as he moved in one motion to cleave off the head of the remaining Knight. The sizzle of skin and the dull thud of a head hitting the ground several yards away was the only noise to be made.

The Shadow Titan turned his head, and stared back into the forest for a moment, looking long and hard into the darkness. Slowly he turned back and continued his way up the road. The Sky Castle loomed large in the distance, another three days' march without rest at least. The immense towers stood tall, even against the backdrop of the mountains, while the great wall that defended the castle wrapped around and into the mountainside, looming nearly a mile high and a quarter mile deep. The wall was made of impenetrable Ethereal Glass or Ether Glass for short, the substance so pure and true, that it could cut through even the darkest of evils. Like clockwork, every two thousand years, when the gravitational nexus of the Light Sun and the Dark Sun crossed paths; two asteroids met the Earth in nearly the same locations. One asteroid landed in the North, in an area known as the Shadow Kingdom. It was enshrouded at all times by deep black clouds and dark, sinister magic known to be used there. Across the realm, there was a decree issued by the Astra King, that these Dark Magic be deemed unnatural and therefore against the natural order. In retaliation, the Shadow King declared war, and unleashed his army on every corner of the realm.

Darkness fell and the rain persisted, yet the Shadow Titan trudged on relentlessly. In the distance he heard the sounds of men, yelling and laughing.

"Fools," he whispered to himself, his attention drawn toward the men. He moved quickly into the shadows of the edge of the forest that lined the road. Eventually, he saw the bright flames of the campfire that this troop of Astra Knights made for the night. He counted at least eight of them, fully armed.

"Salazar," a voice in his head called to him, for that was the Shadow Titan's name. Salazar knelt back into the shadows to listen for further instructions.

"Dispose of those men as discreetly as possible, there are more troops further on down the road and we need to draw as little attention to ourselves as possible."

"Understood." And just as quickly as it appeared the voice was gone, it left Salazar alone in the shadows as he listened intently to the laughter of the Knights, and the sounds of the rain that fell all around him. Salazar moved stealthily through the trees as he circled around the campsite to gain an advantage. Many of the soldiers would be drunk on ale, making it easier for him.

There was a rustle in the bushes behind Salazar, and he whipped around, reacting to the slight sound of a small branch cracking, but there was nobody there.

Salazar refocused on the task at hand, spotting an armed watchguard several yards off. He crouched down low and slipped through the bushes, and within seconds he laid the body of the guard down, throat agape and spewing blood, like a slaughtered animal. The rest of the Knights remained oblivious. Salazar held his hand up toward the group of Knights and before their eyes, their campfire roared to life, from a calm crackling red to a menacing and ominous black that gave off no light. The Knights were instantly sobered, reaching frantically for their swords and armor, but in the darkness it was chaos, and Salazar ran in wildly with two full Shadow Blades. The screams were bloodcurdling and guttural as one by one the Knights were eviscerated, even in the shadows, their blood sprayed violently across the forest, painting the trees a deep crimson. In a matter of moments, it was finished. Salazar sat down next to the fire and drained the last of the horn of ale. The smell of roasted boar drifted invitingly to him and he helped himself to a large helping of meat. The metallic stink of blood and entrails wafted in the air throughout the night, and while Salazar slept, birds, rodents and small foxes cautiously approached to feed on the corpses. On one occasion, Salazar awoke with a start, he scanned through the darkness, but again he saw nothing. Somewhere in the darkness, off in the distance, he made out the faint, yet unmistakable sound of a man running.

It was forty years since the last asteroids fell, and for forty years the realm warred over the precious materials that were harvested from them. This was the furthest that the Astra Kingdom was penetrated thus far, and Salazar was on the verge of reaching the crater. He knew that there would more than likely be another line of defense that he would need to overcome. He waited in the surrounding forest until darkness fell, but no Astra Knights approached the area for hours. Finally, just as Salazar was going to leave his perch, a troop of six armed Knights marched by carrying torches. He crouched in the shadows and listened to them as they passed.

"It's been forty fucking years since this thing has fallen and nobody has been within a hundred miles of here!" one of the Knights complained to the others.

"They are our orders and who are we to disobey them? Besides, it's more peaceful here than being sent out to a battle somewhere against Shadow Knights."

A murmur of agreement came from the troops as they stopped to rest. They unstrapped their belts and lay their weapons down on the ground. Even in the darkness with only the faint, flickering glow from the flames of the torches, their Ether Glass blades resonated brightly. The first Knight used his torch to light up a pipeful of tobakk leaf and he sat back and smoked it thoughtfully before he continued on his rant.

"Do any of you know when the last time a Shadow Knight or any other intruder was seen in these parts?" He continued when none of them replied, "Not since I've been an Astra Knight, that's for sure."

"I'll smoke to that, you can say the same for me," another Knight spoke up, spitting after he toked from his pipe.

The men smoked in silence after that, until their torches nearly burned out. Salazar remained hidden, patiently waiting for any other troops that might come along.

But none came.

Just beyond the clearing where the Knights sat, he could see the humming glow of the Great Crater where shards of Ether Glass still lay embedded in the earth and sparkled like stars across a midnight sky.

An older Knight spoke up then, and the troop all looked, listening with rapt attention. Judging from his voice he was the first that replied to the outspoken Knight.

"You lads better enjoy the quiet while you can; there is something sinister brewing in the North, you mark my words." He nodded with his head over toward a great divide in the mountains. Dark, billowing black clouds crested the skyline in the distance like smoke.

"Only something truly unnatural can cause something as beautiful as the heavens to appear so vile."

"Sir, you speak gravely of the Shadow King and his army, but he has not been seen for many seasons now."

"Not just the Shadow King, young Sir, there are many other evils that lay hidden in those shadows. Some Light, some Dark, some with no allegiance to either."

"Let them answer to this, and we'll see who is hiding in the shadows after that." He held up his Astra Blade, the moonlight reflecting off of it sharply.

The old Knight looked on, smoking his pipe. "Ja, can't argue with that I suppose."

The brash Knight spoke up again, "Come now Karlson, you are being humble in your old age. I have heard all of the stories of you, Shadow Slayer."

"Keep your voice down you fool," Karlson said angrily. "You never know who may be lurking in these shadows."

"If there was a Shadow Knight here I would gut him alive and feed his black heart to my dogs... and wear his tiny shadow of a cock around my neck."

The other Knights laughed at the outspoken Knight's cockiness. All except for Karlson who sat there and shook his head.

"I have seen many Knights finer and stronger than you could ever hope to be young Fredrick, sliced to pieces like they were made of cheese. Those Shadow Blades still keep me awake at night."

Fredrik smiled at Karlson. "Well I know I feel safe with the Shadow Slayer at my back."

The others laughed nervously amongst themselves.

"Well, how about we head back and get ourselves some ale then?" another Knight suggested, finally breaking the tension between them.

"Ja, now that is an idea that I can agree with," Karlson said, as he rose to his feet.

As the Knights began to gather their belongings, Frederik ran over to the forest, only a few yards from where Salazar sat. "Just got to wring out a piss first," he announced, as Karlson watched him with narrowed eyes.

Salazar crept over toward the oblivious pissing Knight and readied his Shadow Blade in his hands. Branches above him shook slightly and caused Frederik to look over. The only noise that followed was the steady stream of urine and once in awhile the soft, muffled whistling of a small bird somewhere in the trees.

Frederik shook off the last drops of his piss, then bent forward to pick up his torch. As his hand reached out for the torch he saw a black blur coming from above. The thud of his arm hitting the ground was the last thing he would hear before the Shadow Blade claimed his head as well.

"Hey, what the hell is going on over there? Frederik?!" Karlson came to check on his fellow knight and stuck his head through the brush. The old Knight stopped in his tracks when he saw Salazar towering over Frederik's lifeless body. Another knight may have screamed, but Karlson was not one of those knights. "You, you do not belong here Shadow Titan. Whoever you are." He spoke calmly and kept his voice low.

Karlson tried to slowly reach to his side where his Astra Blade hung, but Salazar was quick to strike. He rushed toward Karlson, and swung his Shadow Blade down upon the old

Knight within a few strides. The Blade mowed through the thick tangle of the forest easily and slashed Karlson's shoulder, through to the bone. Still, the old Knight grabbed Salazar by the cloak and drew him closer, his grip still tenaciously strong as granite despite his mortal wound.

"I will let you die with dignity, Shadow Slayer. Out of respect of who you are, I will make sure that your head remains attached to your body."

"Salazar, it has been many a season since we last locked blades." His voice gurgled, his throat was trying to stop the blood that flooded his mouth.

"On second thought, I owe you nothing, Astra filth." Salazar sneered, as he withdrew his Shadow Blade and swung it over his head. But before he could bring it down on Karlson's neck, the old Knight unsheathed an Ether Glass dagger from his waist and shoved it deep into the ribs of the Titan. Salazar wheeled and screamed, and dropped the Shadow Blade from his hands. The rest of the troop rushed over to see what all the commotion was about and drew their blades when they saw Karlson keeled over as he gurgled his last gasps. Two of them reacted by dropping their blades, and turned to run when they saw Salazar, in all his glory, burst out of the thick brush wielding two enormous Shadow Blades. In one fell swoop, he swung both blades outwards and slashed the throats of the two Knights nearest him. The pair that started to run slowly came back when they saw Salazar slay the others.

"Sir, if you let us leave, I beg of you we have families and—" With one swing Salazar sliced the Knight in twain from head to toe. The remaining Knight screamed and tried to run again but Salazar swung his blade low and cut the Knight's legs off just below his waist.

Salazar collapsed afterward and grasped painfully at his abdomen. Blood spewed from the wound and his cloak was soaked with it. A tree rustled behind him and he looked back again to see what it was. A small bird whistled from within the branches. Salazar turned his attention back to his wound. He wouldn't be able to continue at this rate without treating it. Again the voice came into his head.

"Salazar, your wound, how bad?"

"I need to treat it, or I will bleed out before I even reach the crater."

"Listen to me, that tobakk leaf those men were smoking, if you can find some, cover the wound with it. Then seal them there with a Black Flare spell. It will burn, and hurt immensely but it will hold the wound closed until we can treat it properly."

"I'll try."

Just then a barely there, yet visible glint appeared at the opening of the forest. Salazar squinted to see what the source was, but it was so small that he could not make it out clearly in the darkness of the night. The light grew stronger and stronger as it approached Salazar, and he readied his blades. From behind the light, the small bird whistled once again.

"Stop where you are! Drop those Shadow Blades!" came the voice of a small child. Salazar retracted his blades into his hands and shielded his eyes from the light.

"Are you lost, child? Why don't you put down that light so I can see you?" Salazar asked.

"You do not belong here," the child replied, and with each step that he approached Salazar, the light burned brighter.

"Who is that?" the voice asked.

"Some lost child, I'll dispose of him shortly," Salazar said quietly.

"Get on with it, we need to reach the crater under the cover of darkness."

The child was now within Salazar's reach. He was a young boy, no older than six or seven years, with a small frame and wild red hair as many children of the mountain region had. Salazar then realized that the light was coming from the short Astra dagger that the boy was holding.

"Put that away son, those are very dangerous to play with."

"I saw you kill those Astra Knights, you must pay for that!" the boy screamed and charged at Salazar, taking a wild swing that barely grazed Salazar's cloak. He charged again but Salazar swung his fist and sent the boy flying back and he landed with a thud against the base of a tree. The boy lost consciousness it seemed and the Astra Dagger tumbled out of his hand.

Salazar rose and kicked the blade aside. He held his Shadow Blade high above his head and swung down hard at the boy's body, but before he made contact, he was blown back by the force of his blade being parried, something shielded the boy. When he gathered his senses, he looked over at the man who appeared out of nowhere. He was short in stature, though most were, compared to Salazar. He wore a dark grey tunic that hid his face and hung loosely around his body like a shroud.

"What is happening, Salazar?" the voice inside his head asked.

"I have no fucking idea, but we are not alone here," he spat.

Salazar drew both his Shadow Blades out and circled the man cautiously. He advanced quickly and swung his blade but the man was too agile, and dodged him easily.

"Salazar, who is that?" came the voice again.

Salazar swung his Shadow Blade again and this time it struck, but the man caught the blade in his own orb of black energy and yanked it completely out of Salazar's grasp. The Blade was gone, absorbed by the man's hands. Salazar swung his other blade down but the man countered with a Shadow Staff from between his hands and blocked it. The man leaped up and swung his staff, striking Salazar directly on the head. Salazar staggered backward, stunned. Again the man quickly set upon him and struck over and over at his legs, arms, and body, anywhere that he could not protect. Amidst the onslaught, the hood of the man's tunic fell back and Salazar finally caught a glimpse of his assailant.

"You—" Salazar tried to speak but couldn't.

"What is happening, Salazar?"

"My Liege, he…"

The man lunged again and swung his Shadow Staff hard and low enough to take the feet out from under Salazar, sending him to the ground with a crash so thunderous, the ground shook.

"What is it? Salazar?"

With the wind knocked from him, Salazar wheezed breathlessly, blood pouring from his mouth as he tried to regain his composure. Salazar panted as he tried to speak before the man sent his Shadow Staff directly through the wound that Karlson stabbed earlier. It penetrated through Salazar's body easily and Salazar screamed as he felt his innards being shredded apart, his entrails swung from the end of the staff that pierced through him.

"Scar..." Salazar sputtered before his lifeless body toppled over to the ground.

About Story Ninjas

Story Ninjas Publishing is an independent book publisher. Our stories range from science fiction to paranormal romance. Our goal is to create stories that are not only entertaining but endearing. We believe engaging narrative can lead to personal growth. Through unforgettable characters and powerful plot, we portray themes that are relevant for today's issues.

You can find more Story Ninja's products here.
Follow Story Ninjas!!!
Website: www.story-ninjas.com
Email: Story-Ninjas@Story-Ninjas.com
Twitter: @StoryNinjas
Youtube: @StoryNinjas